"Are you really here?" she asked, feeling immediately foolish.

"Feels a little unreal, doesn't it?"

She nodded. "I didn't think I'd ever see you again."

He lifted her hand to his mouth, brushing his lips. "I used to have dreams of you. That you were beside me again...sitting close enough that I could feel the warmth of your body by mine. Hear your breathing. And then I'd wake up and—" He let go of her hand and dropped his own hands to his knees. "Doesn't matter. Here you are. Warm and breathing."

She caught his hand, holding him in place. "Don't go."

He looked down at her hand on his. When he spoke, his voice was a low rasp. "Are you sure you want me to stay?"

She knew what he was asking.

"Know what I missed?" His voice deepened. Roughened.

Her heartbeat sped up immediately in response. When she spoke, her own voice sounded breathless. "What?"

"This." He leaned forward, closing the space between them, and touched his mouth to hers.

SMOKY MOUNTAIN SETUP

PAULA GRAVES

HARLEQUIN® INTRIGUE®

For my chat pals, Kelly, Jenn and Donna.
Thanks for keeping me laughing.

Recycling programs
for this product may
not exist in your area.

ISBN-13: 978-0-373-74933-1

Smoky Mountain Setup

Copyright © 2016 by Paula Graves

Printed in U.S.A.

www.Harlequin.com

Paula Graves, an Alabama native, wrote her first book at the age of six. A voracious reader, Paula loves books that pair tantalizing mystery with compelling romance. When she's not reading or writing, she works as a creative director for a Birmingham advertising agency and spends time with her family and friends. Paula invites readers to visit her website, paulagraves.com.

Books by Paula Graves

Harlequin Intrigue

The Gates: Most Wanted

Smoky Mountain Setup

The Gates

Dead Man's Curve
Crybaby Falls
Boneyard Ridge
Deception Lake
Killshadow Road
Two Souls Hollow

Bitterwood PD

Murder in the Smokies
The Smoky Mountain Mist
Smoky Ridge Curse
Blood on Copperhead Trail
The Secret of Cherokee Cove
The Legend of Smuggler's Cave

Visit the Author Profile page at Harlequin.com for more titles.

CAST OF CHARACTERS

Olivia Sharp—In the middle of an ongoing search for traitors in their midst, the last thing The Gates agent expects is for her former love, now a fugitive, to land on her doorstep.

Cade Landry—Disgraced and on the run, Landry's only hope is the woman he thought he'd lost forever. But can he trust her to believe in his innocence?

Alexander Quinn—The former CIA agent who runs The Gates always has his own agenda. Can he be trusted to keep Landry's whereabouts a secret?

The Blue Ridge Infantry—The dangerous militia group held Landry captive for a month and now they're gunning for Olivia. Worse still, they may have allies high in the ranks of the FBI.

Philip Crandall—The FBI assistant director may be Cade's only hope to clear his name. But does he have his own agenda where the BRI is concerned?

Dallas Cole—A visual information specialist at FBI headquarters, he's surprised when a fugitive calls him for help. Will doing what Landry asks put him in danger?

Rafe and Janeane Hunter—The friendly couple who own the Song Valley Music Hall are willing to take in Olivia and Landry when they're running for their lives. Will they live to regret their hospitality?

Chapter One

The ligature marks on his wrists had long since healed, but the stinging phantom pain of the raw spots the shackles had chafed into his skin sometimes caught him by surprise. Odd, he thought, given the other injuries he'd sustained during his month of captivity, that those superficial wounds were the ones to continue tormenting him.

He'd had cracked ribs, for sure. A dislocated shoulder he'd been forced to reduce himself, since the rough men who'd taken him captive hadn't cared much about his comfort.

Cade Landry had escaped on the thirty-first day of his captivity, and he'd been running ever since.

Given the icy chill in the air and the heavy clouds overhead threatening snow, he should have headed south to Mexico instead of wandering around the Southern Appalachians while he tried to figure out what to do next. He could be sipping cerveza on a beach somewhere, flirting with pretty cantina waitresses and soaking up the tropical sun.

It wasn't as if he had any kind of life to get back to now.

And still, somehow, he'd never completely given up on the idea of clearing his name, though he'd spent the past several months avoiding the issue altogether.

No more. It was time to see if there was anything left of his life to reclaim.

Clouds overhead obscured the sun he'd been using as his compass, but he was pretty sure he was still headed west, which would take him out of these mountains sooner or later. Sooner if he was on the Tennessee side, later if he was in North Carolina.

Either way, he was heading for Purgatory.

Where *she* was.

You don't know if you can trust her anymore.

Maybe not, he conceded to the mean little voice in the back of his head. But she was the best shot he had.

He squinted up at the gray sky overhead, enough sunlight still filtering through the clouds to make his pupils contract. Definitely still headed west, he decided, but he hoped he'd reach civilization sooner rather than later. He had to make a stop in Barrowville first. He'd made a point to shave that morning, to clean up and look his most presentable. Maybe he'd get lucky and somebody would give him a ride into town.

The money he'd hidden away before his abduction had still been there when he'd escaped, thank God, but months of living under the radar had taken a toll on his cash reserves. He needed to see if the money they'd put away a couple of years ago was still in the bank. It was a risk, but one he had to take if he wanted to get through the long, cold winter.

Technically, the account was in *her* name, but he was on the account, as well, and as far as he knew, she'd never closed it out.

Maybe it had been as hard for her to let go as it had been for him.

Landry could tell from the color of the sky and the chill in the air that snow was coming, and he'd lived in eastern Tennessee long enough to know that snowstorms in the Smokies could rise up fast, like a rattlesnake, and strike with power and fury.

Just like the men he'd escaped.

OLIVIA SHARP POKED at the fire behind the grate and wrapped her sweater more tightly around her shoulders. Winter in the Smoky Mountains had so far proved to be a cold, damp affair, but tonight they were supposed to get the first snow of the season for the lower elevations.

Growing up on Sand Mountain in Alabama,

she'd seen snow now and then, but rarely enough to blanket everything and shut a person in for more than a day or two. But the TV weathermen out of Knoxville were calling for as much as a foot and a half in the higher elevations, and the lower elevations could expect five or six inches by morning.

She was safe and snug, tucked in with about a week's worth of background checks to read through. In a company like The Gates, which specialized in high-stakes security cases, everything lived or died on the quality of personnel who worked the cases and kept the company running at peak performance, and the CEO, Alexander Quinn, had put her in charge of profiling prospective hires.

She was lucky to still have a job at all, she knew. Her first big job at The Gates had been a spectacular failure. Tasked with finding a traitor in their midst, she'd failed to smoke him out until it was nearly too late. Quinn would have been well within his rights to terminate her employment on the spot, but he'd given her another chance.

She had no intention of screwing up again.

She had made it through three files and was starting a fourth when her cell phone rang. No information on the display, which usually meant her caller was Quinn or another agent who didn't want his identity revealed. "Sharp," she answered.

"Hey, Olivia, it's me." The distinctive mountain drawl on the other end of the line belonged to Anson Daughtry, the company's IT director and one of the people who'd saved her bacon during the investigation into the mole at The Gates, mostly by putting his own ass on the line.

Of course, he'd had a good incentive—the pretty payroll accountant he'd fallen hard for had been right in the middle of the danger.

"I thought you were on your honeymoon."

"I am." She could almost hear him grinning. "Ginny says hi."

"Hi, Ginny." She couldn't stop her own smile. She might like to play the role of a tough woman of action, but two good people crazy in love still had the capacity to make her go all squishy inside. "Seriously, Daughtry, why are you calling me on your honeymoon?"

"You remember that bank account you asked me to start monitoring for activity a few months ago?"

She sat up straighter, the muscles of her stomach tightening. "Of course."

"I got an alert in my email. Someone accessed the account a little after one. Withdrew five thousand dollars."

Olivia glanced at the clock over the mantel. About an hour ago. "Any idea what branch?"

"That's the interesting thing," Daughtry said. "It was the one in Barrowville."

"Oh." A cool tingle washed over Olivia's body, sprinkling goose bumps along her arms and legs. "Okay. Thanks for letting me know."

"Is there anything else you need me to do?"

"No," she said quickly. "I just needed the information."

She could tell from Daughtry's thick silence that he had questions about her request and what the information he'd just imparted to her meant. But she simply said, "Thanks. Go enjoy your honeymoon," and hung up the phone before he could ask anything else.

She could be in Barrowville in fifteen minutes. Ten if she drove fast, although the first flurries had already begun to fall outside her cabin window.

No. He wouldn't still be there an hour later. And the information she needed from whichever bank teller had handled the transaction, she could get over the phone.

She looked up the phone number for the bank and made the call, finally reaching the teller in question after a long wait. "How can I help you?"

"My name is Olivia Sharp. I have an account at your bank." She rattled off the account number she'd memorized ages ago. "I just received an alert that some of the money has been accessed and you were the teller who handled the transaction."

"Yes, ma'am," the teller answered. She sounded young and worried.

"He gave his name as Cade Landry?"

"Yes, ma'am. He had the right identification and he knew the account number. He's on the account."

"I'm sure you handled things by the numbers. I just need to know if you remember what he looked like."

The teller was silent for a moment, long enough for Olivia to fear the connection had been lost. But as she was opening her mouth to speak, the teller answered her question. "He was tall. Dark hair. Nice eyes. I don't remember what color, just that they were nice. Friendly, you know?"

Olivia knew about Landry's nice eyes. She knew their color, as well, a soft hue somewhere between hazel and green. "What about his build?"

"His build?"

"You know—heavy, slim—"

"Oh, right. It was…nice. You know, he looked good." There was a nervous vibration in the teller's voice. "Built nice."

"Athletic?"

"Yes, definitely. He looked athletic."

Olivia closed her eyes. "What about his voice? Low? Medium? Did he have an accent?"

"It was deep, I'm pretty sure. And he didn't have an accent, exactly. I mean, he was from down here somewhere."

"Down here" meaning the South, Olivia assumed. If it was really Cade Landry, he'd have spoken with a Georgia drawl. "I see."

"Is there a problem? Our files show Mr. Landry is still authorized to withdraw funds from the account." The teller was starting to sound worried. "Should I put the bank manager on the phone?"

"No," Olivia said quickly. "Mr. Landry is authorized to withdraw funds. I just wasn't aware he was planning to. Thank you for the information." She hung up the phone and tugged her sweater more tightly around her, trying to control a sudden case of the shakes.

So, someone claiming to be Cade Landry, someone who fit his description and spoke with a Southern accent, had withdrawn $5,000 out of a savings account she'd set up almost two years ago, back when the relationship between her and her FBI partner had been going strong.

Before the disaster in Richmond.

But if it really was Landry who'd withdrawn the money from the account, where the hell had he been for the past year?

THE CHILL IN the air had grown bitter as the cold front rolled in, sending the temperature plunging. Overhead, clouds hung low and heavy, threatening snow.

The bank in Barrowville hadn't given him any

trouble with the withdrawal, so clearly Olivia hadn't removed his name from the account.

Maybe that was a good sign.

He pedaled harder as the newly purchased thrift-store bike started uphill on Deception Lake Road. Getting her new address had been easy enough—he'd asked for and received the latest copy of the bank statement, which included her home address in Purgatory, Tennessee.

It had been a little too easy, really. What if he'd been an ex-boyfriend stalking her?

Isn't that sort of what you are? The mean voice in his head was back.

Fine, he thought. *I'm her ex-boyfriend. And I'm about to drop by her place unannounced. And I'm armed.*

But the last thing he'd ever do was hurt Olivia, no matter how badly she'd hurt him. He just needed to talk to her. He might not be sure he could trust her, but he knew there was nobody else he could trust.

He'd learned that painful truth the hard way.

By the time he reached the turnoff to Perdition Gap, sleet had begun to fall, making crackling noises where the icy pellets hit the fallen leaves blanketing the roadside. He picked up speed as the road dipped downhill toward the narrow gorge cut into the mountains by Ketoowee River, hurried along by the bitter westerly wind that drove sleet like needle pricks into his bare cheeks.

He'd made his choice. Set himself on a course it was too late to alter, at least for today. Snow was coming, and he had to find shelter soon.

And the cabin looming out of the curling fog ahead was his only choice, for good or for bad.

There was a car parked on the gravel driveway, the same sleek black Mazda she'd driven when they had been together. It gave him pause, the sight of something so achingly familiar in a world that had turned alien on him almost two years ago.

He dismounted the bicycle and walked it slowly up the driveway, still staring at the Mazda, noting a tiny ding in the right front panel that hadn't been there the last time he'd seen it. And there was a small parking decal on the front windshield, as well.

The sound of a door opening drew his gaze back to the house.

She stood there in the doorway, dressed in jeans and a snug blue sweater that hugged her curves like a lover. In one hand she held a Mossberg shotgun at her side. He knew from experience that she could whip that thing up and fire before he could reach for the pistol tucked in his ankle holster, so he froze in place.

He realized he could see her better than she could see him. He was bundled up against the cold and damp, a scarf wrapped around the lower part of his face and a bike helmet perched atop his head.

"Hey there, Sharp."

She stopped short.

"Sorry to drop by without calling," he added, moving slowly toward her again, pushing his bike closer to the cabin.

She took a few steps closer to the porch steps, a tall, fierce warrior of a woman blocking the entry. "So it *was* you at the bank."

He stopped at the bottom of the steps and looked up at her. God, she was beautiful, he thought, taking in the perfect cheekbones, the snapping blue eyes and the windblown blond waves framing her face. She'd cut her hair since they'd worked together. The short style suited her.

"It was," he admitted. "I was afraid you'd closed the account, but I thought I'd take a chance."

"Is that how you found me? Through the bank?"

"Your address was on the account."

"And you found a way to get the teller to show it to you." The faintest hint of a smile made the corners of her mouth twitch.

"I did."

She took a deep breath and released it. "But now you've left a paper trail. You have to know it won't take long for people to connect you to me and come looking for you."

"It was a calculated risk." He was beginning to feel a potent sense of unreality, standing here in the cold, gazing at a woman he'd once loved more than anyone or anything in his life.

Sometimes, he thought he still did.

"You should turn yourself in."

"Already tried that," he said bluntly, the heat of old anger driving away some of the cold. "Ended up chained in a backwoods cabin for a month. You'll forgive me if I'm not eager to try it again."

Her eyes narrowed. "Is that supposed to be a joke?"

"No. Believe me, there was nothing funny about it." The phantom sting in his wrists returned. He tried to ignore the sensation, hating the frisson of dread that jolted through him each time he experienced the burning pain.

"You look cold."

He couldn't stop a wry laugh, looking around him at the light snowfall. "You think?"

She made a huffing noise but stepped back, opening a path to her door. "Get inside before you freeze."

He grabbed the used duffel full of thrift-store clothes and climbed the stairs slowly, keeping an eye on her and her Mossberg. She didn't look as if she was inclined to shoot him where he stood, but a lot had changed between them since Richmond.

She entered the cabin, leaving the door open for him. A wave of delicious warmth washed over him when he entered, and he quickly closed the door to shut out the cold.

As he started to turn around, he felt cold steel against his neck.

"Put your hands on the door where I can see them." Olivia's voice was calm and cool. "And spread your legs."

"I'm armed," he warned her as he dropped the duffel bag and complied.

"I figured as much." She started to pat him down, her hands moving quickly over his arms, then slowing as she reached his waist. He couldn't quell a shiver of pure sensual awareness as she slid her hands over his hips. "You've lost weight."

"Meals have been hard to come by recently."

She discovered the pistol stashed in his ankle holster and relieved him of it. "Where have you been?"

"Here and there." He felt her retreat, cool air replacing the warmth of her body. "Can I turn around now?"

"Knock yourself out."

He turned to find her emptying the magazine of his Kel-Tec P-11 onto a rolltop desk by the wall. His duffel bag was on the floor by her feet. "Is that really necessary?" he asked with a nod toward the pile of ammunition.

"For now." She removed the round in the chamber and added it to the pile of ammo on the desk before she set the pistol down and turned her cool blue gaze on Landry. "Why did you come here?"

"Nice seeing you again, too, Sharp. It's been such a long time."

She shook her head, her eyes narrowing. "You disappeared nearly a year ago after McKenna Rigsby's undercover mission went very wrong. At least one corrupt FBI agent has gone missing, and the Bureau is scrambling like crazy to find out what other agents might be compromised. You are on the top of their list."

"I know."

"And yet, here you are. Did you think I would just turn a blind eye to the fact that you're wanted by the FBI for questioning?"

She was magnificent when she was angry. Always had been. Her blue eyes took on an amazing electric hue, and the atmosphere around her crackled with energy. He felt drawn to her, despite himself, and took a helpless step forward. "Livvie—"

"Don't." She held up her hand, a pained look replacing the fire in her eyes. "Please don't call me that."

"I know you have questions. But I've spent the last two hours riding a bicycle in the bitter cold. I'm tired. I'm freezing. I haven't eaten since yesterday. It's snowing out, and I need shelter. Food, if you can spare any. In exchange, I'll tell you everything I've been doing for the past two years, and if you still want to turn me in to the FBI after that, then fine. I'll accept that. Because I'm sick to death of running."

Her forehead creased as she considered what he'd just said. "You'll turn yourself in if I say so?"

He nodded, meaning it. He hadn't realized it until he saw her again, but he really was through running. He'd trusted the wrong person once and lost his freedom for a month—and damned near lost his life in the process.

But he had to trust someone, or what was the point of going on? He couldn't keep living under the radar forever.

And he'd already gone nearly two years without seeing Olivia Sharp. There had been a time when he couldn't have imagined such a thing, couldn't have considered even a week without her, much less a lifetime without her spreading out in front of him as far as the eye could see.

"Were you working with the Blue Ridge Infantry?" she asked, breaking the tense silence between them.

He met her gaze, took a deep breath and answered the question with the truth.

"Yes," he said.

Chapter Two

Hearing Cade Landry admit what she'd spent the past year trying not to believe shouldn't have felt like a kick in the teeth. But somehow, it did. It hit her hard enough that she took an involuntary step backward, her foot catching on the braided rug in the cabin's entry.

As she started to lose her balance, Landry lurched forward and caught her before she could fall, his arms wrapping around her waist. His hands were cold—she could feel the chill through her sweater—but his touch sent fire singing through her blood.

He'd always had that effect on her. Even when he shouldn't.

She pulled free of his grasp, steadying herself by clutching the edge of the desk. "How long?"

He stared at her, a puzzled expression on his face.

"How long did you work for the Blue Ridge Infantry?" When he didn't answer right away, she added, "Are you still working for them? Is that why you came here?"

He took a deep breath and let it out in a soft *whoosh*. "I was never working *for* them."

She shook her head, shock starting to give way to a fury that burned like acid in her gut. "Don't play semantics games with me, Landry."

His dark eyebrows arched, creasing his forehead. "Are you going to listen to what I have to say or should we just cut to the part where you call the cops to come haul my ass out of here?"

"The latter, I think." She went for her shotgun.

He beat her there, jerking it out of her grasp. "Don't," he said sharply as she changed course, going for the P-11 she'd just emptied.

She froze in place, turning slowly to look at him. Something hot and painful throbbed just under her breastbone as she met his hard gaze. "Just get it over with."

"I'm not what you think I am," he said, lowering the Mossberg to his side. "That's what I was trying to tell you."

"You'll forgive me if I have a little trouble believing you."

His lips pressed to a thin line. "I was really hoping you, of all people, would look beyond the obvious."

She pushed down a sudden flutter of guilt. "You don't get to play the victim card. You're the one who disappeared almost a year ago without telling anyone where you were going."

"I did tell someone," he said quietly, lowering the shotgun to the floor, still within his reach. "I told my SAC at the Johnson City RA that I had information the FBI needed to know about the Blue Ridge Infantry. And the next thing I knew, I was being bludgeoned and hauled to some back-woods hellhole and beaten to within an inch of my life."

For a second she pictured what he was say-ing, imagined him tied up and pummeled by the vicious hillbillies who comprised the mountain militia known as the Blue Ridge Infantry, and nausea burned in her gut. She knew from her own investigations that the hard-eyed men who ran the so-called militia as a criminal organi-zation were capable of great cruelty. If they'd ever lived by a code of honor, those days were long past.

Money and power drove them. In these hills these days, money and power too often came from drugs, guns and extortion.

"You told your SAC?" She repeated his earlier statement, trying to remember the name of the Johnson City resident agency's Special Agent in Charge. "Pete Chang, right?"

He nodded. "I didn't think he was corrupt. He's a brownnoser, yeah, so maybe he told the wrong person the wrong thing. I don't know."

"You've been a prisoner all this time?" she asked, looking him over with a critical eye. "Take off your coat."

He looked down at the heavy wool coat he was still wearing, a frown carving lines in his cheeks. "I wasn't a prisoner the whole time," he said gruffly as he unbuttoned the coat and shrugged it off. Beneath, he still wore a couple of layers of clothes—a long-sleeved shirt beneath a thick sweater—but while he looked leaner than she remembered, he definitely didn't look as if he'd been starved for nearly a year.

"Then why didn't you go to the FBI once you were free?"

"I just told you that the last time I told anyone with the FBI what I was doing, I ended up a prisoner of the Blue Ridge Infantry." He pushed the sleeves of his shirt and sweater up to his elbows, revealing what they'd hidden until now—white ligature scars around both wrists.

Olivia swallowed a gasp. It was stupid to react so sharply to the scars—in the pantheon of injuries she'd seen inflicted in this ongoing war between the Blue Ridge Infantry and the good guys, the marks on Landry's wrists barely registered.

It was what they represented—the loss of freedom, the indignity of captivity—that made her heart pound with sudden dread.

Or they could be a trick, she reminded herself

sternly as she felt her resistance begin to falter. He could have inflicted the marks on himself to fool people into believing his story.

The fact remained, he'd just stood here minutes ago and admitted he'd been working with the Blue Ridge Infantry. And nobody who worked with the Blue Ridge Infantry was ever up to any good.

"What are you thinking?" Landry spoke in a low, silky voice so familiar it seemed to burrow into her head and take up residence, like a traveler finally reaching home after a long absence.

She fought against that sensation and gripped the edge of the desk more tightly. "That's really none of your business."

"You're not curious?" he asked, his eyes narrowing as he took a step closer to her. "You don't want to hear all the details?"

She held his gaze but didn't speak.

"Or maybe you really don't give a damn anymore." He spoke the words casually, but she'd known him long enough to recognize the thread of hurt that underlay his comment.

"You're the one who left," she said.

"Are you sure I was the one?" He took another step toward her, and she tried to back away. But the wall stopped her.

"You packed your things and left."

"You'd already left. Maybe not your body, but the rest of you—the part of you that really mattered—" He stopped his forward advancement, looking down at the rough planks of the cabin floor beneath his damp boots. "Doesn't change the outcome, does it? We both walked away and didn't look back, right?"

"Why did you come here?" she asked again, not because she believed he'd answer her any more truthfully than before, but because it was better than thinking about just how many times over the past two years, with how much regret, she'd looked back on the life she and Landry had once shared.

"Because I thought—" He looked up at her, pinning her to the wall with the intensity of his green-eyed gaze. "It doesn't matter what I thought, does it? You've made up your mind about me. I get it." He turned away, heading for the door.

She hurried forward and picked up the shotgun. "I didn't say you could leave."

He turned to look at her. "You're going to shoot me to stop me?"

"If I have to." She sounded sincere enough, even to her own skeptical ears. But her heart wasn't nearly as sure.

She'd loved him once, as much as she'd ever loved anyone in her whole life. Hell, maybe she still did.

If he tried to leave, would she really pull the trigger to stop him from fleeing?

"You won't shoot me," he said softly. "At least, that's what I want to keep believing. So I won't put you in that position."

"You'll turn yourself in?"

He frowned. "I'd rather not. At least, not yet. There's a lot I still need to tell you before you'll understand exactly what we're up against and why."

"What *we're* up against?"

He nodded. "I have to assume someone at that bank in Barrowville will remember the name Cade Landry. And why it's so memorable. They'll call the authorities to report my visit to the bank. And like you said, it won't take long for them to connect us. We were partners, Olivia." He moved toward her, walking with slow, sure deliberation. "Lovers."

His voice lowered to a sensual rumble, bringing back a flood of memories she'd spent two years trying to excise from her brain. "Don't."

"It's too late to undo it, Livvie. I took a risk coming here, and maybe I shouldn't have." He came to a stop just a few inches from where she stood, and she made herself remain in place, though the pounding pulse in her ears seemed to plead for her to run as far and as fast as she could.

Losing him once had nearly unraveled her. If she let him back into her heart—into her bed—again...

"I said I was working with the Blue Ridge Infantry, and that's the truth. But it's only part of it." His hand came up slowly until his fingertips brushed her jawline, sending a shiver of sexual awareness jolting through her. "Did you know they were targeting The Gates?"

She swallowed with difficulty. "Of course. We've been trying to bring them down since Quinn first opened the doors of The Gates."

"I'm not on their side, Olivia. That's not what I meant by working with them—" He stopped midsentence, his head coming up suddenly. It took a moment for Olivia to hear what he'd obviously heard—a car engine moving up the road toward her cabin.

Landry moved away from her and crossed to her front window, sliding the curtains open an inch.

"Could be a neighbor," she said quietly, suddenly afraid he was going to bolt, even though a few minutes earlier, she'd been hoping he'd leave and not look back.

It was just curiosity, she told herself, the need to know what he'd been starting to tell her about his connection to the BRI. It certainly had nothing to do with the way her jaw still tingled where he'd touched her or the quickened pace of her heart whenever she looked his way.

"They're stopping here," he said bluntly, turning back to look at her. She saw fear in his eyes, raw and wild, and realized she had only a few seconds to keep him from doing something reckless.

She pushed past him and looked through the curtains. The truck that had stopped outside her house was a familiar but, under the circumstances, not exactly welcome sight. "It's Alexander Quinn."

Landry groaned. "Your boss."

She looked at him, wondering how much he knew about Quinn. "You said you're not on the BRI's side. Neither is Quinn. If you know anything about The Gates, you have to know that."

"That doesn't mean he's going to turn a blind eye to the warrants out for my arrest."

"You might be surprised."

He shook his head and picked up his duffel bag. "I'm going out the back. Just give me a head start."

She caught his arm as he started past her, not letting go even when he tried to tug free of her grasp. "Don't run. Not yet. My bedroom is through that doorway. First room on the right. Let me find out what Quinn wants."

Landry stared at her as if he were trying to read all the way through to her soul. Finally, the sound of footsteps on the front porch spurred him into action. He went through the doorway and veered right into her bedroom, closing the door behind him with a soft click.

Olivia took a deep breath just as Quinn knocked. *Showtime.*

HER ROOM SMELLED like Olivia, that half-sweet, half-tart scent he'd never been able to identify as anything other than her own unique essence. For a few seconds all he could do was breathe, fill his lungs with that scent, store it away for another drought like the two years they'd been apart since he'd left Richmond—and Olivia— behind.

The bedroom was small and sparsely furnished—a bed, a chest of drawers and a small trunk at the foot of the bed. The bedding was simple and neat—two pillows in pale blue cotton cases, sheets that matched and a thick quilt that looked handmade.

Despite the tension running through him like currents of electricity, despite the muted sound of the door knock just a room away, Landry couldn't stop himself from smiling. It faded quickly, but the flicker of sentiment remained—she hadn't really changed in the past two years if she was still decorating with handmade quilts.

She made the quilts herself, a secret she'd kept from her fellow FBI agents with the ferocity of a mother bear guarding her den. "If you ever tell anyone about this," she'd sworn when she'd finally let him in on her secret, "I will hunt you down and kill you."

The sound of voices drifted down the hallway. The rumble of a male voice, barely discernible, followed by Olivia's alto drawl.

"New bike?" the male voice asked.

"Picked it up at a yard sale," Olivia answered.

Landry pressed his ear to the door, trying to hear the conversation more clearly.

"It's a man's bike," Quinn said in a tone that was deliberately nonchalant.

"I bought it from a man," she answered, a shrug in her voice. "Women's bikes are usually too small for a woman my height."

Good save, Landry thought.

"I got a call from Daughtry," Quinn said, still sounding like someone making small talk. "He said you got a hit on some bank account you'd asked him to monitor."

"That man doesn't know the meaning of *honeymoon*, does he?" Olivia laughed softly, but Landry heard the faint strain of tension behind her words.

Did Quinn hear it, too?

"One of the reasons I hired him," Quinn answered. "But that doesn't answer my question."

"You didn't ask a question."

Still as smart-mouthed as ever, Landry thought.

"Whose account did you ask him to monitor?"

"Mine," she replied. "I've been noticing some discrepancies in my bank statement, so I thought maybe someone had hacked my password for that account. It's not a lot of money, but still."

"So there's someone tapping into your account? Why didn't you just change the password?"

"That would only stop them from accessing the account. I wanted to catch someone in the act."

"Did you?"

"Maybe. I have some feelers out."

Landry didn't hear anything else for several long seconds, not even an unintelligible murmur that would suggest they'd merely lowered their voices. The silence was unnerving. If he couldn't hear them, he had no way of knowing where they were.

Or how close they were getting to his hiding place.

Come on, he thought. *Start talking again.*

"As much as I relish the screwball comedy potential of being snowed in with you, Quinn, you're not going to be able to get that truck back down the mountain if you don't make tracks in the next few minutes."

"Now you're just tempting me, Olivia." There

was a warmth to Quinn's voice that made Landry's gut tighten.

What the hell?

"Funny," Olivia said, but there was no censure in her voice, only a soft amusement that made Landry want to kick down the door.

"Are you sure you're going to be okay here alone? A few of the agents are bunking down at the office for the duration. It's a little college dorm for my tastes, but I think you can handle the frat-boy atmosphere if you'd rather tough it out in a crowd."

"No, thanks," she said with a laugh that was too friendly for Landry's peace of mind. "I'll be fine here. I have a load of résumés to go through and some housework I've put off for the past couple of months. But thanks for the concern."

"Are you sure everything's okay?" Quinn asked in a tone so quiet and intimate Landry had to strain to make out the words.

"Everything's fine."

"Olivia, I know you're blaming yourself for how close Daughtry and Ginny came to losing their lives, but you're not infallible. Nobody in this business is. We all make mistakes."

Olivia's response was spoken too quietly for Landry to hear. But Quinn's next words gave him a pretty good idea what she'd said.

"There are a lot of ways to pay for mistakes.

Sometimes your own conscience is the harshest judge of all. I think you've already given yourself more penance than I'd have ever suggested. That's why I let you come up with your own punishment."

"I would have fired me."

"That's why you're not the boss."

There was another long silence. Landry clenched his fists to keep from reaching for the door handle.

"Call if you need anything. I might know how to get my hands on a snowmobile." Quinn's voice, tinged with amusement, broke the silence, and Landry started breathing again.

He heard the door close and waited until he heard Olivia's footsteps outside the door.

"Still in there?" she asked quietly.

He opened the door to face her. "I was contemplating escape."

"He's gone."

"I heard."

One sandy eyebrow arched over a sky blue eye. "You were eavesdropping?"

"Was there something you didn't want me to hear?"

The other eyebrow joined the first, creasing her forehead. "What's that supposed to mean?"

He meant to change the subject, talk about what a bad idea it was for him to stick around the cabin with her in case her boss decided to come back to check on her in that snowmobile he'd mentioned. But those weren't the words that came out of his mouth.

Instead, to his dismay, he asked, "What the hell is going on between you and your boss?"

Chapter Three

"You were right," Quinn said. "He's there."

Anson Daughtry's voice over the phone picked up a little static as Quinn eased his Ford F-150 pickup around a mountain curve. "What are you going to do about it?"

"Right now? Nothing. She's going to be snowed in with him for a couple of days, and maybe she'll get some information out of him."

"Did you bug the place?" Daughtry's question was delivered bone dry, but Quinn knew his IT director's unfavorable opinion about eavesdropping, especially on employees at The Gates.

"If I did, I wouldn't tell you," Quinn answered just as drily.

"So, you're just leaving her alone with him, without any way of knowing whether or not she might be in trouble?"

"She knows how to call for help if she needs it."

Daughtry made a sound of pure frustration. "Don't you think he's dangerous?"

"I'm *sure* he's dangerous. To someone. The question is, to whom?"

"So you're just letting Sharp find out for you? In a snowbound cabin?"

"If I can't trust my agents to handle themselves in dangerous situations with dangerous people, what the hell am I doing running a security firm?" Quinn had hired Olivia Sharp because everything he'd ever heard about her told him she was perfectly capable of holding her own in a high-risk situation. She'd been a member of an elite FBI SWAT team for six years, and in every dangerous situation he'd put her in since hiring her, she'd proved her mettle. "Sharp is every bit as dangerous as Cade Landry ever thought of being, and she doesn't have any illusions where he's concerned."

"She was involved with him before."

"What makes you think that?" Quinn asked carefully.

"I hear things."

"Then maybe you heard that they're no longer together. And that it ended badly. Which means she's not going to assume his motives for showing up at her cabin in the middle of a snowstorm are entirely pure."

"Love's not that straightforward," Daughtry said bluntly, in the tone of a man on his honeymoon.

"Let me worry about my agents, Daughtry.

You worry about your wife. I'm sure she's shooting you glaring looks by now, considering how long we've been on this call." He pressed the end-call button on his phone and stifled a smile. One of his still-single agents had recently groused that the marriage bug was spreading like a contagion at the office, and Quinn couldn't really deny it.

Take a pair of single, physically fit, energetic and bright people, toss them in the middle of a high-risk, high-stakes situation and step back, because sparks were going to fly. A lot of the time, those sparks fizzled out to nothing once the danger was over, but in some cases, his agents had made real connections with each other, the kind that had a chance to last a lifetime.

Quinn was about as far as a man got from being a romantic, but he'd learned a long time ago not to interfere when a man and a woman wanted to be together.

Very bad things could happen.

OLIVIA STARED AT Cade Landry, certain she'd misunderstood his question. Because there was no way in the world he'd just stood there and asked her what was going on between her and Alexander Quinn, as if it was any business of his. He wasn't a fool or an idiot, and only one of those would stand here in her bedroom doorway, two years after walking out of her life without even a goodbye, and question anything at all about her personal life. Especially in that particular tone of outrage.

But here he was, gazing at her with green eyes blazing with fury, his jaw muscles tight and his nostrils flaring.

"We're going to pretend you didn't just ask me that question," she said in a deceptively soft voice. But she could tell from the troubled look in Landry's eyes that he heard the undertones of danger.

"I'm sorry. You're right. I'm in no position to question anything about your life." He looked down and started to move around her, heading toward the front room.

"Where are you going?" She caught up with him as he was reaching for the unloaded pistol still lying on her rolltop desk.

"I shouldn't have come here."

She caught his hand, stopping him as he started to pick up the pistol. "Why *did* you come here? Why now?"

He looked down at her hand covering his, and she felt the muscles in his wrist twitch as he slowly turned to look at her. "Because I don't know what to do next. And you were always my go-to."

Her heart squeezed into a painful knot. "Even now?"

"Maybe especially now." He eased his hand from her grasp. She made herself let go as he took a step past her, back toward the center of the room. "Maybe it's better we're more like strangers to each other these days. You can be objective about what I should do next."

She couldn't be objective about him, but she didn't bother saying so. She needed to hear where he'd been and what he'd been doing for the past seven months.

"Look, why don't you sit down in front of the fire? You still look cold." She picked up the knit throw blanket draped over the back of the sofa and handed it to him. "Get warm. I'm going to heat you up a bowl of soup. You want a sandwich, too?"

He took the blanket but shook his head. "I didn't come here for you to take care of me." A look of frustration creased his face.

"Then why did you come here?" she asked softly when he didn't continue.

"I needed to see you." The words seemed to escape his mouth against his will. The look of consternation in his green eyes might have been comical under other circumstances.

But Olivia couldn't laugh. She knew exactly what that raw ache of need felt like. She knew what it was like to wake in the middle of the night and feel compelled to reach out for someone who was no longer there beside her. For almost two years, she and Landry had been a unit. Inseparable.

She should have known it would never last. Forever was the exception in most relationships, not the rule. And with her family history, she should never have allowed herself to think she might be able to beat the odds.

"I wish you'd wanted to see me two years ago when I tried to reach you."

Landry looked down, one hand circling his other wrist as if to soothe the scars that formed a circle there. "I should have listened to you when you tried to explain."

"You were too angry."

"I felt betrayed."

Her heart ached at the pain in his voice, but she didn't let herself fall into that morass again. She'd spent too much time blaming herself for Landry's anger when there had been nothing else she could do but exactly what she'd done. "I'm sorry you felt betrayed. But short of lying about what I remembered, I couldn't help you."

His gaze snapped up. "I know. I expected too much."

"You expected me to lie?"

He shook his head. "I expected you to believe me, without question. I thought you would know I was telling the truth, even if you didn't remember."

She stared back at him, guilt niggling at the back of her mind. "I do believe that you remember hearing an order to go into the warehouse instead of holding our position. But that's not what you were asking me to say."

He let out a gusty sigh. "I don't know that I was really asking anything of you except your trust and belief in me. But you never could really give me that, could you? Not wholeheartedly."

Guilt throbbed even harder, settling in the center of her chest. "You know blind trust is a problem for me. You knew that going in." She looked up at him. "I warned you, Landry. And you said you could deal with it."

"Because I thought *you* could." He looked away from her, his gaze angling toward the window beside the fireplace. After a second she followed his gaze and saw that the snowfall was starting to reach blizzard proportion, whiting out everything around the cabin.

"The power probably won't hold out much longer," she warned him, moving toward the hall. "If you want something hot for dinner, we should heat it up while we still have electricity."

He followed her down the short hallway to the kitchen at the back of the cabin. "I don't want to put you out."

"It's soup from a can. I'll heat it in the microwave. You're not putting me out." She pulled a large can of beef stew from the pantry and showed it to him. "How's this?"

"It's fine. Thank you. Can I help with anything?"

"Again, soup from a can, heated in the microwave." She shot him a look of amusement. "Sit down, Landry. You look as if you rode a bicycle here all the way from Bitterwood."

"Barrowville," he corrected her with a wry grimace. "Which was a breeze compared to hoofing it here on foot from North Carolina."

Olivia set the can on the counter and turned to look at him. "North Carolina?"

"I don't want to talk about it right now, okay?" As he met her gaze, waning daylight cast his face in light and shadows, emphasizing how much older he looked now than the last time she'd seen him. The past two years had been hard on him. Aged him, left fine lines around his eyes and mouth.

"Okay," she said quietly and returned to the task of preparing soup for their dinner.

He ate as if he hadn't eaten in days, though, as she'd noticed before, he didn't appear thin enough to have skipped too many meals over the months he'd been missing. Without being asked, she opened another can of soup and heated it up for him.

"Thank you," he told her after he'd finished the second can of soup. "I haven't had anything but protein bars and water for the past two days."

She wanted to ask him what had happened to him, but there was a warning light in his eyes when she leaned toward him, as if he'd read her mind.

She sat back and finished her own soup slowly as he took his bowl and spoon to the sink and washed them. When he was done, he walked past the table and went to stand by the kitchen window to watch it snow.

"How long is the snow supposed to last?" he asked.

"It should snow all night. We should get about six or seven inches, and the temperature isn't going to get above freezing for a couple of days after that. There's a slight chance for more snow day after tomorrow, but the weather guys aren't as sure about that." So he hadn't been near a television or radio in the past few days, either, she noted silently.

Just where the hell had he been all this time?

OLIVIA'S CABIN WAS large and tastefully rustic, but Landry had a feeling the place had come fully furnished. Outside of her bedroom, there was little in the cabin that reminded him of her apartment back in Richmond, a small loft apartment that she'd decorated in cool colors and clean lines. Even her beloved quilts had been stitched together in straight patterns, using fabrics in blues, greens and whites. Uncluttered and organized—that had been the Olivia Sharp he'd known and loved.

But he could tell she'd changed, just as he had. She'd left the FBI first, left him and his anger behind. He'd been both furious and hurt at first, but after what he'd gone through over the past few months, hanging on to resentment seemed pointless.

"I don't have a spare bed."

He looked up to find her standing in the living room doorway, holding another thick quilt like the one he'd seen on her bed. "You have a sofa. That'll do."

She handed him the quilt. It was another of her creations; he could tell by the geometric precision of the pattern.

"Still quilting?" he asked as she started to leave the room.

She stopped and turned to face him. "When I have time. Which isn't often these days."

He set the quilt on the sofa next to him and waved toward one of the armchairs across from where he sat. "You like working at The Gates?"

She sat and folded her hands in her lap. "I do."

"Your boss seems very interested in your welfare."

The look she sent slicing his way was sharp enough to cut.

"Sorry. Too soon?"

"Quinn takes an interest in all of his employees," she said flatly.

"He's trying to take down the Blue Ridge Infantry."

She didn't answer, her eyes narrowing.

"I'm not a traitor, Olivia."

"You never told me how you got mixed up with the BRI." She crossed her long legs and sat back, pinning him with a challenging stare. "I know you tried to help McKenna Rigsby when she was targeted by the Blue Ridge Infantry. You talked to one of our agents, tried to warn him about Darryl Boyle's involvement with the BRI. But one question never really got answered, once you disappeared—"

"How did I know about Boyle?"

"Exactly."

He tried to relax, as well, even though he suspected that some of Olivia's placid composure was an act. He knew his unexpected arrival on her doorstep that afternoon had been a shock to her system, but as usual, she was trying not to let it show.

"I suspected, when Rigsby supposedly went rogue, that something very bad had driven her there. She struck me as a good agent. She sure as hell hadn't joined the Blue Ridge Infantry— she hated them with a passion, hated everything they were doing and how they were twisting things like honor and patriotism for their own purposes." He couldn't hold back a smile remembering Rigsby's tirades. "She vented to me. A lot. She was undercover, trying to get close to some of the female militia groupies, so she had to pretend she thought they hung the moon when she was with them."

Olivia's lips curved with amusement. "She's so not groupie material."

"So you know her."

"I do." She didn't elaborate.

"Is she okay?"

Her smile faded. "She's fine."

"I didn't get to find out what happened to her after she was taken."

"Because you were grabbed by the BRI guys."

God, he hated the skepticism in her voice, the hint of disbelief, as if he'd have disappeared for a year just for the hell of it. "You don't believe me."

"I never said that."

He pushed to his feet. "You didn't have to."

She stood, as well, and caught his arm. "Don't do this. I'm trying to understand what's happened to you."

"You're looking at me as if I'm crazy. Is that what you think?"

"Of course not." Her grip softened, her fingers sliding slowly down his arm to his wrist, where they settled against his scars. "I just need to know why you stayed away so long. Where have you been?"

"After I got away from the guys who took me, I headed east into North Carolina." He gave a little tug of his arm and she let go of his wrist.

"Why east?" she asked.

"Because when I got out of that hovel where they were keeping me, that's the way I was facing. So I ran and didn't look back." He looked down at his scarred wrists.

"Until now. Why did you come back now?"

He looked at her, saw the curiosity in those summer-sky eyes and blurted the truth. "Because you're a target. And you needed to know."

Chapter Four

"That's why you're here? You thought we didn't know we were on the BRI's hit list?" Olivia shook her head, not buying it. "I told you already. We know—"

"I don't mean The Gates is the target," Landry said in a quiet tone that made her chest ache. "I mean *you*, Olivia. The BRI is trying to get their hands on *you*."

She stared at him, trying to read past the mirrorlike calm of his green eyes. "How would you know this? You said you hadn't had anything to do with the BRI since your escape."

"I didn't say that."

She thought for a moment and realized he hadn't. She'd assumed it, given that the BRI had taken him hostage and, according to what he had told her, beaten him terribly to get information out of him.

"Maybe you should sit down and tell me what you know." She waved at the sofa and sat facing him on the coffee table, crossing her long legs under her. "How do you know I've been targeted?"

He leaned forward, resting his elbows on his knees. The action brought him close to her, close enough to touch. All she'd have to do is reach her hand toward him and—

"I got away from the BRI. But I still know some people who lurk around the edges of that group. People who aren't on the inside but are close to men who are."

A cold tingle rippled through her. "Women, you mean. The groupies."

"A couple. Also a few guys who sympathize with the stated goals of the group but don't like their methods or trust that they're what they say they are. There are a lot of people in these parts who've seen the mess government interference has made among their kinfolk and neighbors. You have multiple generations who've known nothing but life on welfare."

"The draw," Olivia murmured. At his quizzical look, she added, "That's what people here call it. 'The draw.'"

"They can't live without it, but some of them hate what it's turned them into, too." He stood up and paced toward the fireplace, leaning toward the heat as if he'd felt a chill. "It makes it very tempting to hook up with people like the BRI."

"I know." She'd grown up poor herself. Had

struggled to escape the cycle of poverty and bad choices that had haunted her family for a couple of generations. "People don't want to feel victimized. Being part of the BRI gives them a sense of power."

"There's a young man I got to know over the past couple of months. Little more than a kid, really. We worked a few day labor jobs together over near Cherokee. His uncle is part of the Blue Ridge Infantry, but this kid is smarter than that. They keep trying to recruit him, but he resists. He's saving up all his money, planning to go to a technical college over in Asheville."

"He's the one who told you the BRI is targeting me?"

"Not exactly." Landry crossed to the coffee table and sat on the edge, facing her. He leaned closer, his gaze intense.

Once again, the desire to reach across the narrow space between them hit her like a physical ache. She curled her hands into fists and kept them in her lap. "Then what, exactly?"

"He got me into a meeting where they were planning their next move in the war against The Gates."

She stared at him. "You were in a meeting with the BRI and they didn't shoot you on sight?"

"Well, they didn't know I was there," he said with a grin that carved dimples in both cheeks, sending her heart into a flip. "The meeting was at his uncle's place, and there's a big vent in the den where they met. My friend lived with his uncle's family for a while when his mama was in rehab a few years ago, and he found out that if you listen through the vent in his old bedroom, you can hear what they're saying in that den clear as day."

"He let you listen in? Does he know who you are?"

Landry shook his head. "I told him I was thinking of joining the BRI because I was tired of how the federal government was taking over every aspect of our lives. He sympathized, but he told me the BRI wasn't the way to go. They were nothing but trouble and he could prove it."

"By letting you listen in on a meeting."

"Yes."

"And you overheard them making a threat against me?"

"Not by name."

"Then how do you know?"

"They called you Bombshell Barbie."

She arched an eyebrow at him. "And that told you it was me?"

"No. What told me it was you was that one of them said you were dangerous as hell and wouldn't go down without a fight. The combination of the two—the nickname and the statement about your fighting spirit—that's what told me it was you."

She stifled a smile, not sure she should feel quite as complimented as she did. "Bombshell Barbie, huh?"

He held up his hands. "I didn't come up with it."

"I know. I'm pretty sure a guy named Marty Tucker did. He was up to his nasty eyeballs in the BRI until he shot himself trying to escape a colony of bats."

"Bats?"

"Long story. He lived. Now he's in state prison, serving time for kidnapping and other assorted crimes. Sadly, he's chosen to keep all his secrets about the BRI to himself, so we're not any closer to bringing them down than we were before." She frowned. "Matter of fact, they've been really quiet recently. No chatter coming out of there at all that we've heard."

"Until now."

"Until now." She cocked her head. "How long have you known about this target on my back?"

"Two days."

"And you didn't think to call and warn me?"

He slanted a look at her. "You'd have believed it was me on the other line?"

"Probably not," she admitted.

"I knew you'd need proof."

"What kind of proof?"

"An audio recording of the BRI's plans."

An electric pulse of excitement zinged through her. "You have that?"

He shook his head. "Not on me. I didn't want to risk getting caught with it. I put it in a safe place."

"Where?"

"I can't tell you that. Not yet."

Her spine stiffened, and angry heat warmed her face. "You can't tell me? I'm the one in danger and you can't tell me?"

His gaze flicked around the cozy room. "How do you know this place isn't wired for sound?"

"I check it periodically for bugs," she said flatly, trying to control her frustration.

"Using what equipment? Something you got from work?"

"Yes." She met his questioning look without flinching, even though she knew where he was going with the question. "And yes, I realize Quinn probably has a way to get around a bug detector he himself supplied. But I trust him with my life."

Landry's eyes narrowed and he pulled back. "Really? Well, I don't."

She bit back a protest and counted to ten. Landry had no reason to trust Quinn, after all. Or anyone else, she supposed, considering what he claimed he'd been through over the past few months. "Fair enough."

"It's safe for now."

"But the BRI is still after me?"

He nodded, easing forward again. "I don't know the timing of what they have in the works. I know only what they're planning to do. What you need to look for."

Another chill washed through her, raising goose bumps on her arms and legs. "Do you mean to keep that a secret, too?"

A small flicker in the corner of his eye was his only reaction to her blunt question. "No, of course not."

"So what do I look for?"

"First, it's not going to be your standard hit. No sniper shot, nothing like that."

She had an unsettling sense of unreality, listening to Landry speak of her impending death as if it was just another case to be investigated. "Is that good news or bad news?"

His gaze snapped up to meet hers. "None of this is good news."

"Right."

He suddenly reached across the space between them, closing his hand over hers. As if he'd read her earlier thoughts, in an urgent tone he added, "This is not just another case for me, Livvie. No matter what happened between us two years ago, you will never, ever be just another case for me."

As she stared at him, heat spreading through her from the point where his fingers had closed around hers, he let go and sat back, clearly struggling to regain his cool composure.

"I'm sorry," she murmured. "Go on."

"They're going to take you when you're alone. So you need to make sure you're never alone."

"That's impossible."

"Look, I know your boss offered you the chance to stay at the office with some of the other agents. Maybe you should do that."

She looked at the whiteout conditions outside the cabin window. "Too late for that."

He followed her gaze. "I'm sure your boss could come up with some way to get you out of here."

She shook her head quickly. "Landry, I'm safe enough here. For now, anyway. I'm armed and it's not easy to get here in the snow. And you're here, right?"

He nodded toward the rolltop desk. "But I'm unarmed."

She met his warm gaze, trying to be objective, to put everything from their past, good or bad, out of her mind and just assess the situation as an agent.

He'd shown up unannounced, after having disappeared for nearly a year, and told her that he'd been working with the same dangerous militia group he now said had made her a target for assassination. But he'd come alone and warned her of the danger against her. He'd had the opportunity to hurt her earlier, when he'd got the drop on her with her Mossberg shotgun, but he'd done nothing to hurt her.

Was he trying to pull some sort of scam? Was this story about hillbilly assassins part of some bigger plan the BRI had hatched?

Or was he telling her the truth?

"Why?" she asked finally.

His eyebrows twitched upward. "Why did I come? I told you—"

She shook her head. "No—why has BRI targeted me specifically? Do you know?"

"They didn't say. At least, not the part of their discussion I was able to overhear."

"What about your friend? The kid whose uncle is a BRI member. Would he be able to find out why they've targeted me?"

"If I could get in touch with him, yes. But that's very dangerous. Even more so for him than for me. He took a big chance letting me sneak in to eavesdrop on the meeting. If either of us had been caught…"

She quelled a shudder as her mind finished the sentence for him, in vivid, brutal images. She'd seen the lengths to which the BRI would go to carry out a plan. "I get it."

"After the snow thaws, I'll see if I can reach him. But I'll have to be very careful."

She pushed to her feet, nervous energy getting the better of her. "There has to be something I can do while we're waiting. Research or something—"

He stood and crossed to her, closing his hands around her arms and pulling her to face him. His expression was fierce at first, but it softened when she met his gaze.

"I'll tell you everything I can remember from what I overheard," he said in a tone so earnest, so familiar, it made her heart ache. "This all has to be confusing and disturbing—"

"Don't do that," she murmured. "Don't handle me."

Slowly, he dropped his hands away from her arms, but the sensation of his touch lingered, making her feel jittery and unsettled. "Let's sit down, okay? Take a second and breathe."

He was still handling her, but at least he wasn't touching her. She returned to the armchair, and he sat on the coffee table in front of her.

So close. So palpable a temptation.

"They managed to get someone inside The Gates—Marty Tucker, I presume—but he was inside before you got there. They don't assume their limited success with Tucker can be repeated, especially since you're still there, sniffing out any possible traitors in your midst."

"How do they know that?"

"They said Quinn's not trying to hide that information. In fact, he made sure it got out

through some of the information channels the
BRI already knows are compromised."

Olivia straightened, alarmed. "Quinn put information about me and my role at The Gates out
there for the BRI to hear? Deliberately?"

"You didn't know?"

She shook her head.

"See why I'm not sure we can trust your
boss?" he asked softly.

She pressed her lips to a thin line, not ready
to speak ill of Quinn to anyone, especially Cade
Landry. But Quinn should have warned her,
damn it! He'd deliberately made her a target by
putting the information out there about her role
at The Gates.

Was her life a bargaining chip in his plan to
take down the BRI?

"He set you up as bait." Landry's voice was
a soft growl.

"*If* you're telling me the truth."

"I am."

She wished she could say she didn't believe
him. But the truth was, setting her up as bait
without warning her was exactly the kind of
thing Alexander Quinn would do. He was always, *always* about the bottom line. Get the job
done whatever it took.

Even if what it took was putting one of his employees in the line of fire to set a trap.

"So they're targeting me? Do they think he won't find someone else to do what I'm doing?"

"They're not going to kill you."

"But you said I was a target."

"You are. But remember when I said they were going to take you? I really meant take you. They're looking to take you captive."

"Why?"

"They seem to think they can use you to break someone."

She frowned. "Someone? Who?"

Landry dropped his gaze, his expression enigmatic as he silently studied his hands for a long moment. When he finally looked up again, an unspoken question darkened his green eyes. "After listening in to Quinn's conversation with you this afternoon, I think they're planning to use you to get to him."

"Why? Why do they think that would get them anything?"

He held her gaze, the questions in his eyes multiplying. "You tell me. I asked you this before, but you didn't really answer. Is something going on between you and Quinn? Are you lovers?"

"No," she answered bluntly. "I mean—"

His eyebrows quirked. "You mean?"

"We're not lovers. But there have been times—" She swallowed with difficulty, suddenly overcome by the acute awareness that Alexander Quinn might have her cabin wired for sound. She took a bracing breath and continued. "There have been times I thought he wanted to be."

"He's in love with you?"

"I don't think Quinn has ever loved anyone that way," she said with a soft laugh. "But he's a man."

"And you're a beautiful woman. Who seems very alone."

She looked up at him. "I choose to be alone."

"Why?" He shook his head. "You're not a loner, Livvie. You enjoy being around other people. You like companionship."

"That was two years ago. My life is very different now. For one thing, I'm too busy for relationships. My job is dangerous and thankless, and I don't want to inflict that kind of stress on someone else."

"Even one of your fellow agents at The Gates? They're working the same stressful job. They understand the long hours, being on call—"

"Why are you pressing this issue? Do you want me to tell you I've moved on from you? I have. It was two years ago." Her voice rose with emotion. "When I left the FBI, I didn't look back. Are you happy?"

"No." He stared back at her, his nostrils flaring. "No, I'm not happy."

She snapped her mouth shut and looked away.

"I know I drove you away. To this day, I don't know how to trust you again, but I have missed you every single moment. The smell of you haunts my dreams. I can close my eyes and conjure up a vivid memory of the sun glinting off your hair that long weekend we spent on Assateague Island. I can feel the thunder of horse hooves beneath my feet when that wild herd ran past us on the beach. I can remember the way your laugh rang in my ears like music."

He hadn't moved an inch closer, hadn't reached out across the distance between them, but his voice caressed her, seduced her, until she felt a throb of desire pulsing low in her belly.

"I didn't come here to get you back. Or ask for another chance," he said in a deep growl that made her think of long, hot summer nights naked in his arms. "But I don't know if I could keep on living if you weren't."

He moved then, rising to his feet and pacing across the room to the window. Outside, the snowfall continued, barely visible in the deepening dusk. Soon night would fall, silent and deep in the snowbound woods.

And she would be alone with the only man she'd ever let herself love.

She couldn't stop herself from rising to join him at the window. He turned slowly to face her, his face half in shadow.

"They're wrong," she said. "The BRI, I mean."

"About what?"

"Alexander Quinn might very well want to sleep with me. He might even feel some level of affection for me. But he wouldn't hesitate to sacrifice my life if he believed it would serve justice in some way. That's the sort of man he is. So if your friends in the Blue Ridge Infantry believe they can use me to control him in any way, they are sadly mistaken."

"That won't stop them from trying."

She lifted her chin. "Let them try."

His eyes narrowed as he held her gaze, studying her as if he'd never seen her before. "You're different," he murmured finally, reaching up to brush a piece of hair away from her cheek. His fingers lingered a moment, and she felt how work-roughened they'd become since the last time he'd touched her that way.

He dropped his hand to his side. "Do you trust me enough to give me back my weapon?"

Trust might not be the right word, she thought, but she was willing to take the risk. "Yes."

He moved away from her to the rolltop desk and retrieved his pistol, reloading it with both speed and skill. "Any chance you have more 9 mm ammo around?"

"Of course."

His gaze lifted to meet hers, a slow smile spreading over his face, carving dimples into his cheeks and taking a decade off his appearance. "Should've known."

As she started toward the hall closet where she kept her extra weapons and ammunition, the lights went off, plunging the cabin into gloom relieved only by the dying fireplace embers.

"There goes the power," she said with a sigh, detouring toward the hearth to coax the fire back to life.

"Wait," he murmured as she reached for the poker. He was much closer than she'd expected; she hadn't heard his approach.

"What?" she asked, her voice dropping to a near whisper.

"How sure are you that the snow caused the power to go out?"

"It's not unusual during a snowstorm—"

He tugged her away from the window. "Or during a siege."

Chapter Five

Only the soft crackle of the smoldering fire and the quiet hiss of their respirations relieved the sudden blanket of silence that fell over the cabin. Outside, snow continued to fall quietly as Landry listened for any out-of-place noises.

Olivia moved away from the fireplace and picked up the Mossberg shotgun leaning against the wall by the desk. She slanted a quick look at Landry before she started toward the front door and grabbed the thick leather jacket that hung on a hook by the entry.

He caught up with her, closing his hand around her wrist. "What the hell do you think you're doing?"

She shook off his grasp and turned to look at him, her blue eyes glimmering in the low light. "I'm going outside to see if I can tell what knocked the power out."

"Didn't you hear a single word I said about a siege?"

"If there are people out there who want to take me captive, I'd rather get the fight over now than hide like a coward in the cabin."

"Well, you're not going out there alone." He chambered a round in the P-11. "I'll go first."

"Why? Because you're the guy?"

He angled a quick look at her. "Because you're the target, and the target should never be the first person out the door."

She frowned but stepped back. "You need a jacket."

He backtracked and shrugged on the thick fleece coat he'd picked up earlier that day at the thrift store in Barrowville, hurrying in case she changed her mind about allowing him to join her.

But she waited for him at the door, her gaze drawing him all the way in as he closed the distance between them. She was a tall woman, nearly as tall as he was, and if anything, she looked even stronger and fitter than she'd been when they'd worked together in the FBI.

They'd always been a good team, right until the case that had broken them. He hoped the old instincts would kick back in for them now, despite all that had passed between them, because if there really were people out there lying in wait for Olivia, it would take all their skills and a whole lot of luck to make it out of the situation unscathed.

An icy blast of air greeted them as they

stepped out onto the cabin porch. Wind had swirled snow beneath the porch roof, depositing about two inches halfway onto the porch's weathered wooden floor.

Landry paused at the top of the porch steps and surveyed the cold white expanse in front of him. If there had been anyone moving around out here in the past little while, they hadn't come close to the porch. The snowfield was pristine and undisturbed.

"The snow probably knocked a branch on a wire somewhere between here and the nearest transformer." Olivia's low voice, only inches from his ear, sent a ripple of pure sexual awareness darting down his spine.

He turned to look at her. "We should check all the way around the house before we let down our guard."

Her eyes narrowed, but she didn't protest as he led her down the steps into the thickening snow. Almost five inches covered the ground, even more gathering at the edges of the porch where the wind had blown the snow into rising drifts. It was a soft, wet snow, flattening under his boots as they slowly circled the cabin, looking for any signs of intruders.

But nothing had disturbed the snow around the cabin, save for a small set of tracks belonging to what he guessed was probably a foraging raccoon, looking for a meal.

"It was just the snow," Olivia murmured, giving him a nudge toward the front of the cabin.

He trudged back through the tracks they'd left in the snow and nodded for her to precede him up the porch steps. She climbed the steps with a soft sigh he recognized as a sign of impatience and turned to face him when he joined her in front of the door.

"Fine," he said. "It was just the snow. This time."

Olivia shook the slush from her boots and opened the cabin door to head inside. He knocked the snow from his own boots before he followed her in.

She closed and locked the door behind him, shrugging out of her damp coat. "Are we going to do this every time you hear a noise you can't identify?"

He tamped down a flood of annoyance. "If I think it's necessary."

She released another sigh as she hung the coat back on its hook. "Okay, fair enough. Let's get the fire cranked up. I'm freezing."

He took off his coat and hung it on the hook beside hers. "How can I help? Need more wood?"

"It's in a bin by the back door. Straight down the hall."

He found the wood bin and grabbed a couple of pieces for the fire then returned to the front room. He found Olivia kneeling in front of the hearth, adding newspaper as kindling to the charred logs still glowing faintly red. He added the wood to the fire and looked around for matches.

Olivia reached into a small steel canister on the mantel and withdrew a narrow fireplace lighter. "Here."

He touched the butane flame to the kindling. It ignited with a soft *whoosh*, and the logs soon caught fire, emitting a delicious wave of heat into the room.

"Nice," Olivia murmured, extending her hands toward the flames.

He pulled the room's two armchairs close to the fire. "Sit."

She did as he said, leaning toward the warmth. "Thanks."

He sat in the chair next to her, holding his icy fingers toward the fire until some of the numbness subsided. "No, thank *you*."

"For what?"

"For extending a little Southern hospitality to a poor, weary traveler?" he suggested with a smile.

Her lips curved in response. "You didn't give me a lot of choice."

"Maybe not. But I am grateful to be here in front of this fire instead of out there in all that cold white stuff."

Olivia fell silent, her gaze directed at the flickering fire. Settling back in the chair, Landry allowed himself to study her profile, take in the lean lines of her body only partially hidden by her sweater and jeans. His earlier observation was correct; she was in excellent shape. She'd always been a curvy woman, and that hadn't changed, but the curves were matched with toned muscles and an overall look of vibrant health.

Leaving the FBI and going to work for The Gates seemed to have been good for her, at least physically.

But what about her spirit? The Olivia Sharp he'd known and loved had been a firecracker, full of explosive energy and a fierce inquisitiveness that had taken her very far very fast in the FBI.

But not this woman in front of him. She was quiet, contemplative and remarkably still.

She stirred as he watched her, turning her gaze to him. "I could heat up some milk over the fire for hot chocolate. Or even water for coffee, if you'd prefer that—"

"You've changed." He hadn't meant to blurt the words aloud, but he couldn't take them back.

Her eyelids flickered and she looked away. "So have you."

Now that he'd started down this conversational path, he decided, he might as well go all in. "Are you happy?"

"I'm…content."

He felt an ache settle in his chest at the hint of melancholy in her tone. "Is contentment enough?"

"For now."

"Do you anticipate finding more than content-ment at some point in the future?"

She slanted a look his way. "Why don't you just come out and ask whatever it is you want to know?"

"Do you miss me?" He clamped his mouth shut as soon as the words escaped his lips. He hadn't intended to ask such a blunt, self-serving question.

"Yes." Her answer, equally blunt, caught him by surprise.

They fell quiet, letting the crackle of the fire fill the lingering silence. Landry wasn't sure how much time had passed before she spoke again, but the flames in the hearth had already begun to die down.

"I loved you. Like I'd never loved anyone in my life." Her gaze remained directed forward, toward the fireplace, the flickering light from the flames bathing her face in a warm glow. "When things fell apart, I had to keep going. Keep work-ing the job, not let the loss derail me. But I just couldn't keep going, day in and day out, work-ing alone when I'd gotten so used to you being there."

The ache in his chest intensified. "I'm sorry."

"You'd been transferred by then. It's not like we'd have been working together anyway."

"I was a mess," he admitted. "It was hard to

care about anything for a long time. I worked the job, but it just didn't mean anything to me anymore."

"I heard you'd started going through the motions."

Guilt flooded him, hot and sour. "I did. Much to my shame. I don't really have an excuse. I just knew I wasn't ever going to get any further up the ladder than I already was, and any screwup would probably be the end of the line for me."

"Easier to keep your nose clean if you're not rocking the boat."

"Yeah. I guess. I'm not sure I gave it that much thought. It's just—nothing meant anything. Every time I cleared a case, three more would pop up to take their place. Bureaucratic crap kept creeping further and further down the line into the field offices. We were dealing with federal-level politics in the Johnson City RA, for Pete's sake."

"Why didn't you just leave the FBI, then?"

"And do what? I spent over a decade solving crimes and protecting lives. It's all I really know how to do at this point."

"You could have come to work for Quinn at The Gates, for one thing." She picked up the fire poker and gave the logs a nudge.

"I wasn't ready." He stopped short as she snapped her gaze up to meet his.

"You weren't ready to work with me again."

"That's not it, exactly."

She turned back to the fire. "Then what is it?"

"I know Ava Trent probably didn't have anything good to say about me. Or McKenna Rigsby, either. But my job was to watch their backs, and I didn't want to leave them in the lurch."

"So you stayed for your partners?" She arched an eyebrow but still didn't look at him.

"I wanted my job to mean something again. I thought if I stuck around, if I did what it took to get through the day, I'd feel that fire again." He shook his head. "As if that fire came from outside of me."

She remained silent for a long time, her singular focus on the flickering fire beginning to make him squirm inside. The Olivia Sharp who'd been his partner, in his work life and his personal life, had been a vibrant force of nature. Quiet contemplation had never been her style.

Maybe that woman really was gone. Maybe he'd lost her in the aftermath of the Richmond debacle just as surely as he'd lost himself.

"I never understood why you couldn't forgive me for not remembering what happened." Her low murmur seemed loud in the snowbound hush of the cabin, yet he was certain he'd misunderstood her.

"What?"

She slowly turned her gaze to meet his, her blue eyes blazing with a mixture of anger and pain. "I had a head injury. I couldn't remember anything that happened right before or right after the explosion. But you seemed to think I should be able to pull those memories out of nothing to prove you weren't lying. That wasn't fair."

"It wasn't what you couldn't remember that was the problem. It's what you told the investigators."

Her brow furrowed. "I didn't tell them anything. I couldn't. I didn't remember anything."

"Yet you somehow managed to remember me pushing you and the other team members to disobey the hold order." His voice sharpened.

"I did no such thing."

He shook his head. Why was she denying it? Did she think he hadn't learned what she'd said in her official statement?

The agents who'd interrogated him had shown him a transcript of her testimony, signed off by Olivia, that had laid the whole mess on his shoulders.

Surely she remembered what she'd told the investigators. The words were certainly burned in *his* mind— "Agent Landry believed that waiting would allow the hostage-takers to escape, so he decided to countermand the official orders and go into the building."

Her eyes narrowed. "What aren't you telling me?"

"Nothing." He was starting to feel sick, his

dinner roiling in queasy waves in his gut. "It doesn't matter."

Her lips flattened with anger. "You're right— it doesn't. The real problem is that you never trusted me. Not really."

How could he argue with her? His lack of faith—in anyone and anything—had long preceded Olivia's presence in his life.

He closed his eyes. "You, of all people, know why I didn't trust anyone easily."

Her fingers closed around his jaw, tugging his face around, forcing him to open his eyes and look into her pain-filled gaze. "I am not her. I never was. I never will be."

He didn't know what to say in response. She was right. Of course she was right. And yet…

She dropped her hand away from his face and turned back to the fire. "We were doomed from the start."

We were, he thought bleakly.

So why hadn't he done the wise thing and walked away before it blew up in their faces?

THE SNOW STOPPED around midnight, but the electricity didn't return. The cabin had been built to keep out the cold mountain winds, but with only the fire in the hearth to keep the place warm, it hadn't taken long for the temperature inside the cabin to drop precipitously.

"This is the last of the quilts," Olivia told

Landry as he sat in silent misery by the fire. Without talking about it, they'd both settled on the thick rug in front of the hearth, huddled together for warmth.

What they hadn't done was speak any more about the past, about the mistakes they'd both made that had led them from the closest of companions to the awkward strangers now sitting side by side under a mountain of handmade quilts.

She'd made it seem that the end of their relationship was entirely his fault, but that wasn't fair, was it? She had her own demons, had made her own mistakes.

"I should have confronted you when you just left without a word."

He made a low, growling sound deep in his throat. "It doesn't matter, does it?"

"I guess not."

He sighed. "I was always a mess. I never should have inflicted myself on you in the first place."

"It never felt like an affliction."

He slanted a skeptical look at her, making her smile self-consciously.

His own lips curved in response. "You can say it. I may be a mess, but I can be honest about my shortcomings."

"I had my own shortcomings. I never felt good enough for you."

He uttered a profane denial.

"No, it's true," she said. "You came from a rich family, and I was from Hick City, Alabama—"

"My rich family left me so screwed up, I walked away from you."

"And my poor family left me so screwed up, I let you go without a fight. Because I'd always figured you'd go, sooner or later." She looked down at her hands, at the short nails she used to wear long and well manicured, and realized so much of the life she'd once lived had been a disguise, a facade she'd invented to make herself feel good enough for the rest of the world. "Little Sand Mountain rednecks like Olivia Sharp don't get to be with rich Savannah boys like Cade Landry. Not for long."

She felt the anger rising off him, as tangible as the waves of heat flowing from the hearth. "You were always the better person, Olivia. You have to know that. You were smarter, stronger, wiser—"

"I never felt that way. And the first time things between us went sideways—"

"I proved you right by walking away," he finished for her.

A soft buzzing sensation from her hip pocket startled her. She'd figured the power outage would have created cell-phone coverage issues, as well, but when she checked the phone display, the signal was strong. "It's Quinn," she said with a glance at Landry.

He nodded at the phone. "Take it."

She answered. "Sharp."

"Quinn," he responded as bluntly. "Is the new bike still parked outside your cabin?"

He knew. She hadn't really doubted he would. "Actually, it's back in the mudroom by the kitchen. Didn't want the snow to rust it."

Quinn sighed. "Damn."

"What do you have against my new bike?"

"Someone's looking for it. Someone with a wallet full of credentials and the full force of the United States government behind him."

Damn it. "You're not suggesting I put the bike back out in the snow to fend for itself?"

Quinn dropped the games. "Landry's a wanted man. If the FBI tracks him to your place—and given his little trip to the bank in Barrowville, it's really only a matter of time before they do—things could get very uncomfortable for you both."

She looked at Landry, who was watching her with troubled eyes. "Any suggestions?"

"I realize travel at the moment is hardly optimal, and you should have at least another couple of days, because the FBI isn't likely to try to make it up the mountain before the snow thaws. But if I were in your place, I would be planning not to be there by the time the roads are passable again."

"Understood."

Quinn hung up without saying goodbye. She closed her own phone and shoved it back in the pocket of her jeans.

"Something's happened," Landry said.

"The FBI is looking for you here in Tennessee. Quinn doesn't think they've tracked you to the bank in Barrowville yet, but it's only a matter of time."

Landry pushed to his feet. "I'll get out of here."

She scrambled up, catching his arm as he reached for his boots. "They won't come tonight. Or tomorrow, most likely."

"That'll give me time to get far away from here."

"Don't," she said, her heart suddenly pounding wildly.

He looked down at her fingers closed around his forearm. "Don't what?"

She swallowed hard, forcing the words from her tight throat. "Don't leave me behind again."

Chapter Six

"Forget I said that." Olivia took a step back and let go of his forearm, turning away.

Landry didn't let her retreat. Not this time. He closed the distance she'd opened up, until the heat of the fireplace filled what little space remained between them. Its glow bathed her face with gold and added sparkling glints to her blond hair. Desire snaked through him, but he ignored its sibilant seduction. Wanting her wasn't enough. It had never been enough.

Maybe that had been the problem. Wanting was easy. Visceral.

Trusting—that was the hard part.

"I can't forget you said that." He laid his hand on her shoulder, keeping the touch light and undemanding. But her gaze snapped up to meet his, her blue eyes darkening with arousal as if he'd caressed her.

He still had that effect on her, just as the mere sight of her made him long for her touch.

"This is a mess of my own making. You're not part of this. I can go, and you can pretend I never darkened your door."

"I can't pretend that." She looked away quickly, as if she could hide the desperation her eyes had just revealed. But it was too late. He'd seen the fear. It echoed the same desperate emotion burning in the center of his chest.

Need. Pure, unadulterated need.

He needed her. His partner. Set aside everything else—the desire, the complicated history, the perceived betrayals and the two-year separation—and the partnership remained, a connection between them that time and distance hadn't been able to sever after all.

"You were a good agent," he said. "A damn good one, actually. And I need my partner one more time, okay? I won't deny it. But it's still your choice. I'm not a good bet here. I'm in a mess and I can't even offer you ironclad proof that I'm telling you the truth."

She turned slowly to face him. "I believe you."

Her simple declaration jolted through him like an electric shock. "Livvie—"

She held up her hand. "I believe you came here to protect me. That's what I believe. But I'm going into this with my eyes open. And the second you keep secrets from me and tell me a lie, that's it. I'll know it. And you'll be out there on a shaky limb all by yourself, because I'll be going to the FBI and telling them everything I know. Including your last whereabouts."

He couldn't hold back a smile of relief. That was the Olivia Sharp he'd known and loved, the tough-minded, no-nonsense agent who'd watched his back and saved his ass more times than he could count.

"Fair enough," he said, holding his hand out to her.

She looked at his outstretched fingers for a tense moment then clasped his hand in hers and gave it a firm shake. "I think we're safe here until morning. So let's pack up the supplies we're going to need to hike up the mountain in half a foot of snow and then get some sleep so we can head out before daylight."

He should have known she'd have a cabin full of survival gear and supplies. Olivia Sharp had set the standard for preparedness during her years in the FBI field office in Richmond. She already had a prepared "bug out" kit, as she called it, containing camping supplies, tools and a 72-hour supply of Meals Ready to Eat as well as changes of clothing.

She had a second backpack stored in the hall closet. Within a half hour, she'd added another three-day stock of supplies and food to that back-pack, as well, filling in the blanks with clothes from his duffel bag.

"The cold will be a pain, but these hills are

full of places to find shelter," she said in a tone that was all business. He mimicked her brisk attitude as he carried the two backpacks to the front room and set them near the fire while she retrieved extra weapons for them, adding a compact Glock 19 to her Mossberg and handing over a spare pistol.

He looked at the Kimber Stainless II pistol in his palm and smiled. "You remembered."

"It was two years ago, not two decades," she said in a flat tone. "It's loaded, and I put extra ammo in your kit. Now let's try to get some sleep before morning, okay?"

She settled down on a bed of quilts and pillows that had been warming by the fire while they'd gathered supplies, her back to Landry.

He tucked the Kimber in the borrowed backpack and sat down beside her on the makeshift bed. "We should sleep back to back," he said, glancing at her quilt-covered form.

"Knock yourself out," she murmured.

He stretched out beside her and covered himself with a quilt, as well, easing back until his body collided with hers. "Sorry."

"Shut up and go to sleep, Landry."

Stifling a smile, he tucked the quilt tightly around him and closed his eyes. There were only a few scant hours before morning, and they both needed as much sleep as they could muster.

But he had a feeling, no matter how few hours

remained between him and dawn, this was going to be one of the longest nights of his life.

DAYLIGHT WAS STILL an hour or two away, nothing more than a faint gray glimmer in the eastern sky, when Olivia woke. The fire had died down to warm embers, allowing a bone-aching chill to settle over the cabin's front room. Only the solid wall of heat pressed against her back kept her from shivering and burying herself more deeply beneath the two quilts covering her from chin to toe.

The hot body behind hers shifted and uttered a familiar groaning sound that made her breath catch in her throat.

Landry.

"You awake?" His voice was like rumbling thunder, muffled by the quilts.

"I am."

He shifted, turning over until he was practically spooning her. "I think my fingers fell off during the night. Can't feel them."

She rolled over to face him. His green eyes met hers with sleepy humor, and she felt something hot and tight release inside her, allowing her to breathe deeply again. "You'd better find them," she said with the hint of a smile. "You're going to need them."

He brought his hands out from beneath the

quilt and touched her neck. His fingers were like ice.

She batted them away, laughing despite herself. "Stop!"

"Cold hands, warm heart."

Her smile faded. "We need to hit the road soon."

He sighed. "If we can find the road."

They ate a breakfast of protein bars and left the cabin while it was still mostly dark out. As Olivia had hoped, once they got past the clearing around her cabin and into the woods, the snow was thinner on the ground, thanks to the shelter of the trees overhead.

"Keep an eye on the trees," she warned as Landry fell into step behind her. "Limbs can snap without a lot of warning."

"Duly noted."

She'd tasked him with hauling the crude travois she'd fashioned from a rake handle, a hoe handle and a canvas tarpaulin, which she'd loaded with the supplies she'd packed into a waterproof duffel in case they had to find shelter before they reached their destination.

"What is our destination, exactly?" Landry asked as they headed deeper into the woods.

"Well, for tonight, I want us to reach a place called Parson's Chair." When he didn't say anything else, she turned to look at him. "No comment?"

His green eyes narrowed as he met her gaze. "I

come from Georgia. I have no standing to make fun of strange place names."

She smiled. "It's a tall outcropping that kind of looks like a tall, straight-backed chair, hence the name. But beneath the chair is a large cave that will give us shelter if we can reach it by nightfall."

"And if we can't?"

She turned and started walking faster, tugging her jacket more tightly around her. "Let's just make sure we do."

PARSON'S CHAIR WAS near the top of Fowler Ridge, the southernmost peak of the two mountains that flanked Perdition Gap. On a warmer day, with good weather, Olivia could reach the outcropping within a three-hour hike. She and a couple of the female agents at The Gates had made the hike several times over the summer.

But climbing the winding natural trail in subfreezing temperatures, with a slick carpet of snow underfoot, was turning out to be a grueling test of endurance. She had nearly fallen once already, and as she neared the halfway point of their hike, she heard the sound of a hard thud and a guttural curse behind her, turning in time to see Landry slide almost ten feet back down the mountain on his side, the travois he was pulling tumbling with him.

She reached for the end of the contraption,

where she'd strapped the poles together, and caught it before it went over the side of the trail, keeping a sharp eye on Landry as he struggled out from beneath the travois and regained his footing. As he crawled back up the mountain, she held out her gloved hand to him, and he grasped it with a grim smile of gratitude.

"Clearly, I don't have any pack-mule DNA in my ancestry," he muttered as he joined her near a clump of boulders.

She shrugged her backpack off her shoulders and settled on one of the smoother rocks. "Let's rest a minute. Rehydrate and warm up." She pulled out a thermos of warm broth she'd stowed in the backpack before they'd left the cabin that morning.

Landry settled on the boulder beside her, retrieving his own flask. They drank in silence for a few moments before he closed the flask and put it back in his pack. "How much farther?"

She looked at him and saw with alarm that he was wiping blood from the side of his face with the sleeve of his jacket. Rising quickly, she eased his hands away to get a better look at the injury. It was a nasty scrape that started in the middle of his cheek and went into his hairline, disappearing under his black ski cap.

"It's just a scratch," he protested.

"It's bleeding like crazy," she growled, grabbing her backpack to find the compact first-aid kit she'd put inside.

"Seriously, it's a scratch. My head's not even hurting." He winced when she pressed an antiseptic pad against the scrape.

"The travois is obliterating our tracks, for the most part, but if you're leaving a blood trail, I'm not sure the snow we're supposed to get tonight is going to be enough to hide it."

He closed his eyes. "And we're about to spend the night in a cave."

"We're not unprepared."

He opened his eyes, giving her a curious look. "When did you learn all this doomsday prep stuff, anyway?"

"I was born with survival skills," she murmured, mopping up the blood from his face. The scrape continued oozing, but it wasn't as bad as the bleeding had made it look. She tucked the used wipe into a disposal bag and shoved it back in the pack, then made quick work of applying adhesive bandages along the length of the scrape. "All better."

He caught her hand as she was about to let it drop away from his face, pressing her palm against the day's growth of beard scruff on his jaw. Dimples flirted with his cheeks. "But do I still have my boyish good looks?"

He was flirting with her, the beast. And worse,

she was falling for it, hard. Damn his charming hide.

She tugged her hand free of his grasp and picked up the first-aid kit. "You're assuming you ever had boyish good looks."

He put his hand over his heart, feigning injury.

She put the first-aid kit in the backpack and swung it up on her shoulders. "We should get moving again if we want to reach Parson's Chair before nightfall."

She didn't wait for him to gather his things before she started hiking up the trail again. Behind her, she heard the sounds of his scrambling to catch up, and she took a little pity on him, slowing her pace until he had.

"You've developed a cold side." His voice drifted to her on the icy wind.

"I've always had a cold side."

As the trail widened, he moved up until he was walking side by side with her. "Not like this. Is it because of me? Because I'm not worth it."

She slanted a look at him and saw he was serious. "Trust me when I say you are only a single line on a lifelong list of reasons not to let myself be vulnerable to other people."

"You never talked much about your past."

"It wasn't important."

"It should have been." He caught her wrist as she continued forward, forcing her to turn and face him. "I should have asked."

"It doesn't matter," she said, tugging free of his grasp once more and continuing up the mountain. What was done was done, and there wasn't a thing either of them could do to change it.

Snow started falling again late in the afternoon, a blizzard of tiny flakes at first, creating a fine mist that looked like the tendrils of mist that gave the Smoky Mountains their name. But within an hour, the flakes grew larger and the snowfall thicker, reducing visibility to almost nothing.

Landry had no idea how they'd be able to find Parson's Chair when they couldn't see ten feet in front of them.

"Stay close," Olivia called, her voice almost whipped away by the wind.

"Wouldn't dream of letting you out of my sight," he muttered.

After what felt like another hour of hiking, though a glance at his watch told him only fifteen minutes had passed, Olivia slowed to a halt. "There it is," she said.

He followed her gaze and saw the faint outline of a rocky outcropping visible through the wall of falling snow. "Parson's Chair?"

"Let's go," she said, hiking forward at a reinvigorated pace.

Tightening his grip on the travois, he followed, ignoring the ache in his calves and thighs. When they finally reached the mouth of the cave beneath Parson's Chair, he eased the front of the travois to the ground and stretched his sore limbs. "Remind me to hit the gym more often when I get back to civilization."

She shrugged off her backpack and shot him a look of amusement. "And here I was thinking you were looking lean and ripped."

"That's from walking everywhere I went, hauling around a backpack and eating only a couple of meals a day." He eyed the dark opening of the cave. "Any chance there's a bear inside?"

"They'd be hibernating at this time of year anyway."

"I heard black bears don't hibernate."

"Why don't you take this, go in there and find out?" She handed him a flashlight from her backpack and waved her hand toward the cave entrance.

"Gee, thanks." He took the flashlight and took a step inside, swinging the light in a slow arc to get his bearings.

The cave was larger than he'd expected, a cavern about twenty feet wide with a high ceiling. The back of the cave disappeared into darkness, suggesting there might be a tunnel that went even farther into the mountainside.

"Any bears?" Olivia's voice was right in his ear, giving him a start. He hadn't even heard her approach.

"If there are, they're hiding." He shone the flashlight in her face, making her squint.

"Give me that." She took the flashlight and headed back outside to grab her gear. He joined her, unloading the travois and helping her take their supplies deeper into the cave.

He had to give her credit; she'd prepared well for a night in a cave. The well-packed duffel he'd been dragging behind him on the travois contained a portable propane heater, two fleece-lined sleeping bags and extra bottled water. "You forgot the portable toilet." He slanted a sly look her way.

She waved her hand toward the cave entrance. "The toilet came with the accommodations."

"Yeah, I've used it before." He folded one of the sleeping bags into a square and sat cross-legged in front of the duffel bag, looking through the rest of the supplies. "No wonder that bloody thing weighed so much. You packed half your cabin."

She followed his example and folded her own sleeping bag into a makeshift seat cushion. "I wasn't sure how long we'd have to be out in the elements." She opened a bottle of water and took a drink.

He grabbed his own bottle of water. It was icy cold, which might have been good about six months ago when he was living through the hot North Carolina summer, but now served to add chills on top of his existing shivers. "How long does that heater last?"

"Six to twelve hours, depending on the heat level. I figured we'd start as low as we can so we can make it last longer. These sleeping bags will help. And we should probably change into dry clothes now, too."

"You want me to wait outside?"

She met his questioning look with one arched eyebrow. "I don't think either of us grew anything new since the last time we saw each other naked. I know I haven't."

He smiled at that as he stood up. "I'll turn my back anyway."

"Chicken," she murmured.

His grin faded as he heard the zip of her jeans and struggled to keep a memory of her sleek curves and warm golden skin from taking over his brain. After shucking off his own wet clothes, he pulled on the jeans and sweater he'd stashed in his backpack. The dry clothes warmed him immediately.

"All done," Olivia said.

Turning, he shook the melted snow out of his hair and used his discarded sweater to soak up some of the remaining moisture. "You became quite the Girl Scout while we were apart. I used to beg you to go camping, with very little luck, and here you are earning your merit badge in disaster prep."

"There's a difference between knowing how to survive in the wilderness and actually wanting to do it for recreation." She settled on her sleeping bag again and took off her boots and damp socks. Her toenails, he noted, were neatly pedicured and polished a bright sky blue that seemed to reflect the azure tint of her eyes. "Hopefully, we won't be up here more than one night."

He sat next to her on his own sleeping bag and followed her example by taking off his snow-stained boots. His socks were still mostly dry, so he didn't take them off. While she donned dry socks and another pair of boots, he asked, "Why *did* we come up here, anyway?"

"Because it's halfway to where I want to go. And I knew we could find shelter here for the night."

"And where is it you want to go?"

She stopped in the middle of tying her boot and looked up at him, her expression hard to read. "We're heading for The Gates."

Chapter Seven

"I thought you didn't trust Quinn."

The words, spoken quietly but urgently, were the first words Landry had uttered since she'd told him of her intentions to hike to The Gates for refuge. She had expected resistance, and when he'd merely turned away from her and started sorting through the rest of the supplies to see what food was available for supper, she hadn't known what to think.

The Cade Landry she'd spent almost two years of her life loving had been quick-tempered and just as quick to get over it. But she wasn't sure this slow-simmering version was an improvement.

"I don't trust him to put my safety above whatever mission he's running at any given time," she admitted, taking the MRE he was holding out to her and reading the packet label. "Spaghetti. Discriminating choice."

He managed a smile, though she could tell

he was still disturbed by the thought of putting his own safety—and freedom—in the hands of Quinn and the agents of The Gates. "Eat up. It's going to be another long hike into Purgatory tomorrow, right?"

She sighed. "I know you're not happy about going to The Gates, so you can stop pretending that everything's fine."

"What's the point? You're going to go whether I do or not. And since it's your life in danger, I can't exactly let you head off there alone, can I?"

"Why not?" She dropped the MRE on the cave floor in front of her and angled her chin toward him, her own anger rising in a rush. "You had no trouble leaving me behind two years ago, did you?"

"Maybe we should talk about who left whom."

"Maybe we should."

For a moment tension crackled between them like a live wire. Olivia's chest started to ache from the hurt and anger she'd kept pent up for too long. But was a cave in the middle of a snowstorm really the place to have this argument?

"I'm sorry," she said, picking up the MRE she'd thrown down. "This isn't the time or place—"

"You'll tell me when you find that time and place, right?" he asked in that quiet tone she was beginning to recognize as his slow boil.

"Do you really want to hash this out here and now?"

"No," he admitted. "Not here or now."

"Let's just get some food and some sleep, in that order." She opened the MRE and pulled out the packets inside. The entrée was the first place to start, she decided. The most calories, and she could eat it hot. She could save the items that didn't require heating for breakfast. "You know how to use one of these things, right?"

"Yeah." He picked up the flameless ration heater. "Been a while, though."

"These come with saltwater packets to activate the heater." She poured the water into the heater, activating the chemicals that produced heat. The packet warmed quickly, and she held it as long as she dared, until the heat began to sting her fingers. She shoved the entrée into the heater packet and set it aside. "What sides came in your packet?"

He went through the small packets that had come in his meal. "Cheese and crackers, fig bar, shortbread cookies, raisins—"

"Trade you my peanut butter for the cheese spread, and this yummy oatmeal cookie for the shortbread." She waggled the packets at him.

"Deal on the cheese spread, but I don't know. These shortbread cookies sound pretty appetizing." He held out the packet toward her, pinning her with his gaze. "But I might be convinced to trade it for something else."

Despite the icy chill of the cave, the air between them heated instantly. The familiar fire in his gaze was pure temptation, and damned if she didn't want to tumble in headfirst.

She looked away. "If you want the shortbread cookies, keep them."

He let out a little huff of air. "Here. You can have them. I'll take the oatmeal cookie." He laid the packet of shortbread cookies on the cave floor in front of her.

She looked up and saw something in his expression she hadn't expected.

Sadness.

"Landry—" She stopped. Started again. "Cade."

His eyes snapped up at her use of his first name. "You never called me Cade when we were together. No need to start now."

"Maybe that was a mistake. I mean, you called me Olivia. Why did I have to put that distance between us?"

"That wasn't what put distance between us." He looked down at the shortbread cookies she hadn't yet picked up. "And it wasn't just you. I need you to know that I know that I was a big part of the problem."

"Maybe we were just too damaged for anything between us to have a chance to work." To her dismay, she felt hot tears stinging her eyes, threatening to fall. She blinked hard, keeping them at bay.

"I wish I wasn't in this situation." He growled

the words, his voice deep with frustration. "I wish I'd just come to you before, when there weren't people hunting for us both. I wish I'd told you that I loved you and we could figure out a way to make it work."

"I could have tracked you down and said the same thing." She made herself look at him, to face the choices she'd made. "I wasn't ready to make that move, and I wouldn't have been ready to give you a second chance if you'd shown up at my door, either."

"Then why don't I feel like it's really over?" The words seemed to tumble from his lips, fast and desperate, as if something inside him was determined to get the question out before his better judgment found a way to shut him up.

"I don't know," she answered as truthfully as she could.

"You don't feel that way, do you?"

She could lie, she supposed. Tell him what he clearly believed to be the truth. But she'd never been able to lie to him with any effectiveness.

"I do," she admitted, forcing herself to say it. Get it over with. "I do feel that way. I never felt as if we got any closure, the way it ended. You know?"

He nodded. "I know."

"I need you to know. I really loved you. Like I've never loved anybody in my whole life. And when things fell apart, I felt ripped in two." She couldn't stop the tears, as much as she wanted to. She pushed them away with her fingertips, shooting him a watery smile. "Sorry. I know you hate it when I cry."

He reached across the space between them, the pad of his thumb brushing a tear from her cheek. "I know you loved me." He dropped his hand away. "You just couldn't believe in me."

"You said that before. When you first showed up at my cabin yesterday. You said I just couldn't believe in you enough. But I don't know why you think that. Is it just because I didn't tell the panel that I remembered getting an order?"

"No, of course not." He looked puzzled by the question. "I knew you had a head injury, so I get that you might not have remembered the order."

"Then what did I do that was so unforgivable?"

"It's what you told the panel about my obsession with the BRI."

Now she was the one who was confused. "What?"

"Olivia, it's okay. Maybe you were right. Maybe I was getting a little too focused on bringing them down. I mean, look at the mess that obsession has gotten me into now."

"But I didn't say—"

"Peterson sneaked me a copy of the transcript of your debriefing. I read your statement."

She shook her head. "There's got to be some

mistake. I mean, yeah, I was still suffering from the concussion, but I remember really clearly what I told the investigation team, and I didn't say anything like that about you."

"But your statement—"

"Either you misread it, or you didn't see the real transcript," she said firmly, anger rushing heat into her cheeks. "Because I never said anything like that to the debriefing team. Concussion or no concussion."

"How can you be sure? If you had a head injury, maybe you said things you were thinking that you wouldn't have said aloud if you weren't suffering a concussion—"

"I know I didn't say it, because I never thought it. I never thought you were obsessed with the BRI. You were passionate about bringing them to justice, yes. But so was I. We both wanted that group of terrorists stopped."

A look of dismay crossed his face. "Then if you didn't say it—"

A chill washed over her that had nothing to do with the snowy weather outside the cave. "Someone falsified my deposition."

"But who?"

"Peterson's the one who gave you the sneak peek. Could he have changed it?"

"I guess he could have, but why would he? He'd gain nothing from it. He wasn't on the SWAT team that day." Landry rubbed his chin, his palm making a soft swishing sound against his beard stubble. "Who was in the debriefing with you?"

She frowned, trying to remember. "Definitely the squad leader, O'Bannon. Agents Thompson and Lopez of Internal Affairs."

"What about Darryl Boyle? Was he there?"

She met his urgent gaze. "Yes. He'd been the unit leader that day."

"I've been thinking a lot about that day in Richmond. I've gone over it and over it in my head, replaying every second."

"I wish I could remember."

"No. You don't. I never thought I'd say this, but I'm glad you don't remember." He looked queasy. "You don't remember two of our friends—our brothers—blown up in front of us."

She reached across the space between them, touching his hand. His gaze snapped up to hers, but instead of pulling away, he covered her hand with his own.

"I'm sorry. I'm sorry I wasn't well enough to attend the funerals for Davis and Darnell. I should have been there with you."

"I missed you," he admitted, giving her hand a light squeeze before he pulled away and rose to his feet. There was a faint glow of lingering daylight coming from the mouth of the cave; he walked toward it slowly until he stood in the opening.

She tugged her jacket more tightly around her and followed, stopping next to him in the cave opening. "Snow's starting to slow down."

He glanced at her. "How much more do you think fell?"

She gazed into the gloom, making out only faint impressions of their trek to the cave in the snow. "At least three or four more inches. Looks like maybe nine inches altogether."

With a little shiver, he turned and walked deeper into the cave. "How long before we can turn on the heater?"

"I'd like to wait until we bunk down. Let's eat. The food should be heated by now, and that should warm us up for a bit."

He lowered himself onto the folded sleeping bag and reached for the box holding his MRE.

"Use your—"

He growled an oath and dropped the now-open box on the cave floor.

"Glove," she finished.

"Thanks for the warning." He slipped on his glove and fished the hot entrée out of the box while she did the same. Steam rose from the packets, filling the air around them with the smell of food.

They ate in silence from the entrée packets and drank a whole bottle of water each before stowing away the trash for disposal when they reached town the next day. Outside, night had descended, snuffing out almost all the light from the world beyond the cave.

"I want to get a predawn start tomorrow," she warned as she handed him the flashlight. "Here, hold this where I can see what I'm doing with this heater."

He pointed the flashlight beam toward the small propane heater. "Is it dangerous to run that thing in an enclosed space like this?"

"It shuts off automatically if the oxygen level gets too low." She made sure the fuel tank was safely seated in place. She turned on the power, and heat rose from the vents. "Plus, this cave has an opening deeper inside. If you wet your finger and hold it up, you'll feel the breeze."

His lips curved and his dimples made a quick appearance. "I'll take your word for that."

"We should probably try to sleep with our backs to the heater," she suggested as she unfolded her sleeping bag and laid it out by the unit.

He followed her lead, setting up his bag on the other side of the heater. "How much more battery time does that flashlight have?"

"Should be plenty for the trip. But let's not waste it." She switched it off, plunging the cave into inky darkness.

For a few minutes, the sounds of movement, hers and his, filled the silence as they unzipped their sleeping bags and slid inside, then zipped themselves up within the fleece-lined cocoons.

Silence reigned again for a long while, broken only by the soft whisper of their breathing and the hiss of the propane heater warming the air between them.

"I'm sorry." His voice rumbled in the darkness a long time later, just as she was starting to relax.

"For what?" she asked, resisting the temptation to turn over to face him.

"For being reckless. Getting that money out of our joint bank account yesterday, even though I knew it was possible—probable—that the account would have been flagged."

"So why did you?"

"I guess I was just tired of being out there alone," he said after a long pause. "I missed having someone who gave a damn about my life, and since you were the last person who really did—"

"I'm not sorry," she said quietly.

When he didn't respond, she wondered if he'd heard her.

"I'm not sorry," she said more loudly, turning her head to make sure he could hear her. "I've been so worried about you, for a lot longer than just the time you've been missing. I'm glad you came to my cabin. I'm glad I know you're okay."

"For now."

She sighed, turning her back to him again, suddenly overwhelmed by a heavy sense of danger creeping closer.

"For now," she conceded and closed her eyes,

giving in to the bone-aching weariness from a day's hike up the mountain.

She didn't think she'd fall asleep easily, despite her fatigue, but the comforting flow of warmth from the propane heater and the soft, steady cadence of Landry's breathing soothed her into deep, dreamless slumber.

LANDRY OPENED HIS eyes and stared into the black void of the cave, listening to Olivia's slow, steady breathing. It felt a little ridiculous, really, to be forcing himself to stay awake just so he could listen to her sleep nearby.

That was how much he'd missed her. Enough that something as simple as hearing her move oxygen in and out of her lungs was the most comforting sound he'd heard in two long years.

Why had he let her go? His reasons had seemed so right, so overpowering, in the heat of his anger and the burning humiliation of what he'd perceived as betrayal. But he believed her now when she said she'd told only the truth.

He should have believed it all along. He should have told her what he'd read and heard her side of the story. She'd have told him the truth, that she hadn't painted him as an unstable obsessive, and then maybe—

Maybe what? Maybe they'd still be together?

He'd have found a way to screw it up. He'd never had a relationship last longer than a few months before Olivia. Looking back, he wasn't sure how she'd put up with him as long as she had.

Maybe her own emotional baggage had made her more patient than she might have been. She'd come from poverty, from an unstable home with a young and irresponsible mother. Her father had been little more than a stranger, and while she'd sworn nothing terrible had happened to her during her childhood, he'd begun to suspect her father's behavior with her when she reached her teens had made her uncomfortable.

"I was lucky," she'd said firmly the one time he'd brought the subject up. "My mom might have been a major mess as a parent, but she never let anyone hurt me that way. Besides, after I hit my teens, we moved away from Sand Mountain, and I never saw him again."

He hadn't said what he'd been thinking, that maybe her mother had chosen to leave their hometown behind to get her away from her father and his discomfiting behavior.

Whatever the reason, he was glad she'd got out of that situation mostly unscathed.

But she hadn't got away without emotional baggage, any more than he'd escaped his own troubled youth without deep and lingering trust issues.

An unfamiliar sound drifted toward him

through the inky darkness, dragging his mind out of the past and back into the cold, uncertain present.

Not unfamiliar, he realized as the noise came inexorably closer.

Just unexpected.

Footsteps approached the cave at a slow, steady pace, crunching the crusty snow underfoot.

They had a visitor.

Chapter Eight

Consciousness returned to Olivia in a nerve-rattling rush, leaving her disoriented. Something had awakened her. But what?

"Don't make a sound." She recognized Cade Landry's voice, quiet but urgent. "Someone is moving around outside the cave." His voice was little more than a whisper of breath against her cheek that time.

She tried to sit up and realized she was cocooned in her sleeping bag.

She heard the faint sound of a zipper, and cold air flooded over her, scattering goose bumps across her skin. Wriggling free, she rose to her feet.

Cold steel pressed against her fingers. Her Glock 19. She didn't bother to check the magazine—she'd loaded it before they left the cabin.

"How do you know someone's out there?"

As if in answer, she heard the crunch of boots in the snow outside. She went very still and silent, her nerves instantly on high alert.

Landry touched her arm briefly then moved toward the mouth of the cave, staying out of the semicircle of faint illumination that lightened the cave floor just in front of the entrance.

She joined him there, just a few feet from the world outside, peering through the darkness for any sign of movement.

"Do you see anyone?" She felt his question more than she heard it, a huff of warm breath tickling her ear.

"No."

Suddenly, shockingly close by, a male voice uttered a low oath.

Next to her, Landry's body reacted with a slight jerk. She put her hand on his arm, recognizing the voice. "It's okay. I know who it is."

"Sharp, if you're in there, I think I just broke my damn ankle." The male voice outside spoke in a whisper.

With a sigh, she started toward the cave door.

Landry caught her arm, jerking her back against the hard heat of his body. "Are you crazy?"

"I told you—I know who it is."

"It could be a trap."

"It's not a trap," came the voice from outside, sounding both pained and annoyed.

She pulled free of Landry's grasp and went outside. Sitting on a low boulder nearby was a lean man with spiky brown hair and a pained look twisting his feral features. He had one leg crossed over the other, massaging his ankle through the hiking boot.

"Hammond, what the hell do you think you're doing up here in a snowstorm?"

Seth Hammond made a face. "I could ask you the same thing."

She shot him a pointed look and he shrugged.

"Rachel and I bought a place just up the gap from where you live. I took the baby out to see her first snow and I spotted two idiots climbing up the mountain in a bloody blizzard. One of 'em was dragging something behind him like a pack mule. So I went and got my binoculars. You can imagine my surprise when I saw one of those idiots was you."

"Funny."

"Anyway, I thought I should see what you were up to. And who was with you."

She sighed, looking at her colleague from The Gates. "What if I didn't want you to know what I was up to and who I was with?"

He eased his foot to the ground. "Well, the good news is, I don't think I can hike down the mountain to tell anybody what I saw. I'll probably just sit here and freeze to death, and nobody will ever find out what you're up to."

"Do you really think it's broken?"

"It's not broken." Landry stepped out of the cave, taking up a protective stance close to her.

"You would have screamed when you put your foot down on the ground that way if it was broken."

Seth peered up at Landry through narrowed eyes. "You a doctor?"

"No. I'm a guy who's had a broken ankle."

Seth pushed to his feet, testing the injured limb. He seemed to be holding his weight easily enough. "What do you know? It's not broken."

"Told you it was a trap," Landry muttered to Olivia.

"It wasn't a trap." Olivia looked pointedly at Seth. "Did Quinn send you?"

"No. I told you—I saw you from my house."

"You're not seriously trying to sell me that story."

The look on Seth Hammond's face was pure innocence. "Would I lie?"

She rolled her eyes. "Uh, yeah, you'd lie. You were a con artist for years. It's kind of what you do."

"Con artist?" Landry asked.

"Reformed," Seth said with a feral grin.

"Or so he says." Olivia glanced at Landry. "Think we should just leave him out here? Since he's not crippled or anything?"

"Oh, come on, Sharp. It's damn cold out here, and I think I hear the sound of a heater running in that cave."

"Should have packed your own," Landry said.

Seth gave him a considering look. "Don't believe I got your name."

"Don't believe you did," Landry agreed.

"Might as well let him get warm or he'll sit out here whining all night and keep us awake." Olivia nodded for Seth to enter the cave ahead of her.

Landry caught her arm as she started into the cave after Seth. He kept his voice low. "I don't like this."

"He's a colleague at The Gates."

"I don't care. I don't trust anyone at The Gates except you."

"But I do. And we're going to need help if everything you've told me is the truth."

"Of course it's the truth."

"Then we don't need to try to go up against a whole army of well-armed, morally bankrupt rednecks by ourselves."

Seth's voice wafted out of the cave. "Got any extra MREs in here?"

"No," Olivia and Landry called in unison. She looked up at him, struggling against a smile.

He didn't fight it, grinning down at her, his dimples making an appearance that even the dark night couldn't quite hide. "I don't know, Sharp. You and I always made a pretty good team. Just the two of us."

She took a step back from him, alarmed by the sharp tug of longing that gripped her by the heart. "There hasn't been just the two of us in a long time."

His grin faded. "You trust your buddies at The Gates, but you don't trust me."

"*You* don't trust *me*," she countered, lowering her voice further. "That was always our problem."

"I guess it was," he conceded. "And it went both ways."

She couldn't argue. "But maybe it's not too late to learn to have a little trust in each other." She glanced toward the cave. "I'm telling you, Seth Hammond is a lot of things, but he's not a traitor. He takes his work at The Gates very seriously, and part of his work is watching the backs of other agents. Including me."

"So you're asking me to trust your judgment about a man who claims he hiked who knows how many hours up this mountain just to see what you were doing?"

She couldn't stop a soft huff of laughter at his dry tone. "Yeah. I guess that's exactly what I'm asking."

He looked toward the cave entrance then back at her. "That's a hell of a lot to ask, Sharp."

"I know."

He sighed. "Okay. Fine. We'll let the huckster join our slumber party."

"Reformed huckster." Seth's voice drifted out from the cave.

"Ears like a bat," Landry murmured. "Kinda looks like one, too."

"I heard that."

"Shut up and grab yourself one of those protein bars," Olivia called to Seth. "But keep your mitts off my MREs."

Landry nodded for her to come with him, a little farther from the cave. She followed, trying to hide her growing amusement at his irritation. When they reached the edge of the rock formation that formed Parson's Chair, he stopped and turned to look at her.

"You don't think he really just spotted us hiking up the mountain and took it upon himself to follow us all the way up here on a whim, do you?"

"I'm not an idiot."

"So what do you think? Quinn had him staked out to watch your place?"

"Maybe. Or more likely, he's tracking us electronically in some way."

"You mean GPS?"

She glanced back toward the cave. "Some of the equipment I brought with us came from The Gates. I guess there could be trackers inside some of them."

"Quinn tracks his agents? He doesn't trust you?"

"We had a problem with leaks. We had a mole in the agency, and Quinn's very touchy about it. So for a while, he was tracking all the agents to see where they went. I guess it's hard for him to let go of his CIA instincts."

"So the hillbilly con man in there might be removing all the trackers while we're out here chatting?"

She shook her head. "No. Quinn doesn't care if I find out about the trackers. He's making a point to me with them anyway."

"And that point would be?"

"I might be one of his agents. I might even be one of the ones he's most likely to confide in. But he's never going to fully trust me. Or anyone else."

"Sounds like a couple of people I know."

She made herself meet his gaze. Now that her eyes had adjusted to the dark, she could make out the details of his familiar face, the lean planes of his cheeks and the curve of his full bottom lip, a hint of softness in his otherwise chiseled features. She couldn't make out colors, but she knew from experience that his green eyes held a touch of hazel, shifting hues with his emotions. Right now, she knew, his eyes would be a deep, smoky green, like a forest pool reflecting the earthy colors around it. A hue of green she'd learned long ago meant he was troubled and tense.

"It's freezing out here. Why don't we go back into the cave?" She lowered her voice to an intimate murmur.

He slanted a look at her. "Right now, hearing you talk to me in that tone, I'm really wishing your good buddy the con man wasn't waiting for us in that cave."

She felt a jolt of pure sexual thrill whip through her body like electricity. She'd forgotten how easily he'd been able to seduce her out of a bad mood or a fit of anger. One soft, oblique hint of desire in that sexy growl of a voice, and she was on fire from the inside out.

"Landry—"

He smiled, sighed and gestured toward the cave. When he spoke, his voice was soft with understanding. "Come on. Let's get inside before he eats all our food."

LANDRY HADN'T EXPECTED to get much sleep with a stranger sharing the cave with him and Olivia, but her sense of ease must have been contagious, for he was asleep nearly as quickly as she was and woke to morning light seeping into the cave and the sound of a whispered conversation taking place close by.

"Of course he sent me." That was Seth Hammond's quiet drawl.

"He doesn't trust me?"

"He doesn't trust sleeping beauty over there."

"Landry's not a danger to me."

"Are you sure about that?"

There was a brief pause before her answer, long enough for Landry's stomach to tighten.

"Positive," she answered, and even in a whisper, conviction rang in her words. "He needs my help. I didn't know how to give it to him before, but I'm not going to stop this time until we figure it out."

Deciding to stop his eavesdropping while he was ahead, Landry rolled over and made a low, sleepy groaning sound as he stretched.

"Good morning," Olivia said.

He turned to look at her and his breath caught. Her face was free of makeup, her hair was a tousled mess, but she was still the most beautiful thing he'd seen in ages, and even the presence of Seth Hammond didn't keep him from wanting to cross to her and take her to bed right there on the icy cave floor.

He managed to control the urge and pushed up to a sitting position. "No more unwanted visitors while I was asleep?"

"No, just me," Seth said with an unperturbed grin. "Let's just get this out in the open, okay? I know who you are. I know the FBI is looking for you. And I know Olivia here doesn't think you're one of the bad guys. And since my track record with the authorities isn't exactly clean, I'm in no position to judge your decision to run instead of turn yourself in."

"How did a guy like you ever get a job with The Gates in the first place?" Landry grabbed his jacket as an icy draft raced through the cave, making him shiver. Olivia had already turned off the heater, and most of the residual heat had dissipated.

Olivia tossed Landry his half of the leftovers from their meal the night before. "Eat some breakfast. We can talk about Quinn's hiring practices later. We need to get on the trail again."

"At least it's downhill from here," Seth said in a cheerful drawl that made Landry want to throw his breakfast at the man.

Instead, he examined the packets Olivia had tossed to him. Peanut butter and crackers, a toaster pastry, raisins and an oatmeal cookie.

"Yum," he muttered.

"Food is fuel," Olivia said briskly as she started rolling up her sleeping bag. "Eat up. Daylight's burning."

HIKING DOWNHILL IN the snow wasn't a lot better than hiking uphill, Landry decided a couple of hours later as he hit a slick patch and landed hard on his tailbone. The impact knocked the wind out of him for a moment, and the poles lashed together at the pointed end of the travois cracked hard against his chin.

Olivia and Seth both stopped to help him back up. "You want me to pull the mule cart for a while?" Seth asked, nodding at the travois with a friendly grin.

"Let him do it," Olivia told Landry in a dry tone, already heading back onto the trail. "Serves him right for letting Quinn turn him into his personal bloodhound."

Landry handed over the travois poles and caught up with Olivia on the trail. "Are you sure heading into town is the best idea? Quinn clearly doesn't trust me or he wouldn't have sent your huckster buddy back there to make sure you were okay in my company."

Hammond's voice piped up behind them. "Reformed—"

"Shut up!" Landry and Olivia snapped in unison.

Olivia slanted a quick look at Landry, her lips curving in a half smile. "I don't know if it's the best idea," she admitted, her smile starting to fade. "But it's the best one I have. You have any better ideas?"

"No," he had to admit.

"At the rate we're going, we should hit town in about two hours. Then the pace should pick up because the streets are relatively flat, and you won't be tripping over hidden stones every few yards."

"What's between here and town?"

"Enemy territory," Hammond said, his voice closer. He'd caught up with them despite his heavier load.

"There's a small enclave of people who claim allegiance to the BRI," Olivia explained. "Their cabins are a little ways off the trail, so if we're lucky, we shouldn't have any trouble with them."

Landry caught her arm and stopped her in her tracks. "If we're lucky?"

"It snowed nearly a foot up here in the mountains. Power up this way is spotty on a good week, so they're probably hunkered down, trying to stay warm. It'll be all right."

"You hope."

"I expect," she said firmly. But he saw her grip her Mossberg shotgun more tightly as she started hiking forward again.

They walked awhile in silence before Olivia broke it with a soft question. "Where is your evidence?"

So much had happened between the time he'd shown up at her cabin and this laborious hike down the mountain, it took Landry a moment to understand what she was asking.

"Evidence?" Hammond prodded when Landry didn't answer immediately. "Evidence of what?"

"Of the BRI putting a hit out on me," Olivia

answered in a flat tone that belied the feral alertness behind her blue eyes.

"It's not a hit exactly," Landry corrected her.

"So they interrogate me roughly for a few days before they put me out of my misery. Close enough to a hit for me," she said.

"Wait—what?" Hammond wriggled out from under the travois and trudged forward to join them. "Someone's trying to take you prisoner, and you're out here hiking into town by yourself?"

"She's not by herself," Landry protested.

Hammond shot him a hard look. "Close enough. Why didn't you tell Quinn? He could have put a half dozen agents on your place to stand guard."

"So then I'm Quinn's prisoner instead."

"At least Quinn's not looking to put a bullet in your brain," Hammond snapped, all of the folksy humor gone from his demeanor. "Damn it, Sharp, why do you always play it this way? Why don't you let anybody help you?"

Landry looked from Hammond to Olivia, taking in the bristle of anger in her expression and the frustration in Hammond's voice. Apparently, this wasn't the first time Olivia had clashed with her fellow agents at The Gates about her lone-wolf attitude.

He guessed a few things about Olivia hadn't changed in the past few years after all.

"Let's just get to your office and get warm." Landry nodded at the travois Hammond had dropped. "You can call Quinn and tattle on her when we get there."

The sharp-eyed look Hammond threw Landry's way would have intimidated a different man. But after all that Landry had gone through over the past few months, it would take a hell of a lot scarier man than Hammond to make him flinch.

Hammond released a harsh breath and stalked back to the travois.

"You want me to spell you for a bit?" Landry asked as the other man jerked the lashed poles over his shoulders.

"I'm good," Hammond growled.

"You have such a way with people," Landry murmured to Olivia as he caught up with her.

"I don't want people at the agency thinking I need to be wrapped in cotton and put away somewhere safe."

"Do they do that as a rule?"

She cut her eyes at him. "I haven't tested the theory yet."

"If you're so worried that's what's going to happen, why are we going to The Gates in the first place?"

Her voice rose. "Because I have nowhere else safe to go, okay?"

They walked on in silence for another half

hour, battling a rising wind that whipped up the mountain, blowing snow around them and limiting visibility to a few dozen yards. The watery sunlight that had offered a brief reprieve against the icy chill had faded behind a sheet of low-lying clouds that threatened more snow.

"What was the forecast the last time you checked?" Landry asked. He'd lost his cell phone months ago and had never bothered to replace it. Whom did he have to call? But he'd seen Olivia checking her phone that morning before they hit the trail.

"It might snow a little more," she answered. "They weren't sure."

"How much more?"

Coming to a sudden stop, she didn't answer. Landry followed her gaze into the blowing snow and saw what she'd seen. Movement, straight ahead.

There was someone out there in the woods ahead.

"How close are we to the BRI enclave?" Landry asked softly.

"Too close," she answered.

Behind them, Seth Hammond uttered a soft expletive.

"Well, now," came a low drawl, "look who just wandered into our territory, boys."

Landry froze, a flash of images flooding his

memory so hard and fast he felt as if he'd been gut-punched.

He knew that voice. He'd heard that voice every day for a month, the deceptively gentle tones that had been a sound track for the brutality of his henchmen.

He'd never seen the face—they'd made sure of it. But he'd know that voice anywhere, even in his nightmares.

Landry turned slowly, bracing himself for his first look at the monster who haunted his dreams.

But before he could move, a crack of rifle fire split the icy air, and he threw himself at Olivia, shoving her to the ground beneath him.

Chapter Nine

The idiot was trying to protect her!

But in the process, he'd damn near knocked the Mossberg out of her hand. She shoved him off her and rolled onto her stomach, leveling the barrel toward the last place she'd seen their gun-toting intruders.

But they were gone, running through the snowy woods like wraiths, fading into the white-washed scenery.

As Olivia turned her head to check the rear, Landry pushed her down again, his weapon hand whipping toward a spot behind her. "Don't move."

"Landry—" Hammond began.

"Shut it," Landry barked. "Put the guns down."

"You're outnumbered." The familiar voice sent a shudder of relief ratcheting through her body. She shoved Landry off again, ignoring his growling order to be still, and looked up to confirm what she'd heard.

Six men in arctic camouflage stood in a semi-circle around them, eyes alert and rifles raised. One man was clearly in charge, a dark-haired man with dark hazel eyes and lean, chiseled features. He wore the camo like a second skin, which made sense, she supposed, given his decade in the US Army.

"They're friendlies," she said sharply to Landry, putting her hand over the hand that held his gun.

"Says who?" he growled, shoving her hand away.

"I say," she said firmly, circling to stand between his pistol and her colleagues. The second she got a look at his wild-eyed expression, a quiver of pure terror ripped through her gut. In that moment, she realized, he could just as easily shoot her as not.

Then his gaze focused on her. His expression softened a notch, and he slowly lowered the Kimber to his side.

"Friendly to whom?" he asked, his voice raspy and unsteady.

"To me. And you." She held out her hand to him.

For a moment he looked at her as if she'd lost her mind. But she didn't budge.

After a long, breathless moment, he turned the Kimber grip toward her and handed it over.

She slid the Kimber into the waistband of her

jeans and turned to face the men from The Gates. "You should have brought Ava," she said to the leader. "He knows her."

"Yeah, well, she and Solano are down in Alabama. Solano's sister had her baby a week early." Sutton Calhoun shrugged and nodded toward the men flanking him. "Somebody go help Seth out. He's too damn scrawny to be a pack mule."

Hammond made a rude gesture at Calhoun, earning a laugh from Calhoun and the other guys on the squad. But he stepped forward and gave Sutton a downright brotherly hug. "How'd you know to come to our rescue?"

"We didn't. We just knew from your last text that y'all were heading down the mountain in the morning, so we figured you might run into trouble here in the redneck red zone. Quinn asked for volunteers, but when nobody spoke up, he made us draw straws." Calhoun grinned. "We got the short ones."

"Funny."

"This him?" Calhoun nodded toward Landry but looked at Olivia for a response.

"What, you don't have my mug shot hanging on the office wall?" Landry's sarcastic tone almost hid his underlying tension.

Almost.

"I'm Sutton Calhoun." Calhoun extended his hand.

Landry ignored it.

"Manners," Olivia murmured.

He looked at her as if she'd lost her mind. When he answered, his coastal Georgia drawl kicked in. "This ain't a cocktail party, darlin'."

Calhoun shrugged and finished the introductions. "This is Fitzpatrick to my right. That's Dennison on the left. Cooper's the big guy. Jackson's the guy on the end."

"And I believe we've spoken before." Nick Darcy stepped forward.

"You answered the pay phone at the Econo-Tel," Landry said, showing the first hint of relaxing. "The guy with the British accent. You were protecting Rigsby."

Darcy nodded. "You probably saved her life with that call. If we'd been even a few steps behind Darryl Boyle—"

"Olivia says Rigsby's okay."

"She's splendid," Darcy answered in a tone so besotted, Olivia couldn't quell a smile.

"I see," Landry murmured, glancing at Olivia.

"We probably shouldn't stick around here much longer," Calhoun warned. "Those fellows might have gone for reinforcements."

"Don't suppose you brought any skis with you?" Hammond muttered.

"You can't ski worth a lick anyway," Calhoun said, clapping his friend on the back before barking an order in the sharp tone he must have learned during his days in the Army. "Move out."

THE LITTLE TOWN of Purgatory looked like a Christmas card, covered with snow and sparkling with lights in the deepening twilight. The temptation to stop his weary trudge forward and just enjoy the sight was more than Landry could resist.

He'd been in and out of civilization over the past months, slipping into bigger towns when he needed supplies or information, but most of his time had been spent in the hills, bunking down wherever he could find a kind soul who would take pity on his homeless state and give him a hot meal and a place to stay for the night.

He hadn't stayed overnight in a town since he'd got away from the BRI, and he'd begun to wonder if he ever would again.

"Can't linger." That was Sutton Calhoun's voice, gentle but firm in his ear as he nudged Landry forward. "We're almost home."

"Home," it turned out, was a deceptively shabby-looking mansion on a large, tree-shaded corner lot near the center of town. An engraved plaque near the large iron gates read "Buckley Mansion, est. 1895." A smaller, less ostentatious sign on the gates themselves, however, proclaimed that they'd arrived at The Gates.

"Why The Gates?" Landry asked Olivia as they entered through the iron portal and started up the snowy walk.

"I'm not sure," Olivia admitted.

"The gate of purgatory," Dennison offered as he passed them on the way to the front porch. "Though some of us think it's the gates of hell instead. Occasionally."

It looked like heaven to Landry, welcoming lights glowing warm in the windows, though when they walked inside, the front lobby was empty. But there was light and blessed heat, and an instant sense of safety, however transitory it might prove to be. The temptation to relax his guard was almost more than Landry could resist.

"Who else is here?" Olivia asked.

"Rigsby's here," Dennison drawled. "You know Darcy—never leaves home without her. Brand is up with Quinn at his office."

"Delilah's working the storm shift?" Olivia asked.

"Along with Sara and Ivy."

"Sara's Dennison's wife—Ridge County sheriff's deputy," Olivia told Landry. "Delilah and Ivy are married to Brand and Calhoun, respectively."

"They're both local cops over in Bitterwood."

"Y'all have some sort of law-enforcement dating service going on the side?" Landry asked softly as Olivia led him to the winding stairway leading to the second floor while the other men headed out of sight, shedding their outerwear as they went.

She smiled. "Easier to date someone who gets

your crazy hours. You should know that better than anyone."

He did. Of course, he and Olivia had shared most of those crazy work hours, which could have been a problem, he supposed. But somehow it never had been. Work was one part of their shared lives that had never been an issue.

Until Richmond.

He put the dark memories out of his head and followed Olivia down a dimly lit hallway to a room at the eastern corner of the house. She gave a soft knock but didn't wait for a reply before she entered.

A sandy-haired man in his forties sat behind a large oak desk, leaning back in his chair with his hands steepled over his chest. He looked up, unsurprised. "You're an hour later than I expected."

Olivia sighed. "We ran into a couple of BRI boys. Slowed us down."

"Everybody unscathed?"

"I'm sure Sutton or someone on the team has already texted you the details," she drawled, nodding at the other man in the room, a tall, darkhaired man with blue eyes who had turned at the opening of the door. "Brand."

Landry froze. "You're Adam Brand."

Brand's dark eyebrows lifted. "And you're Cade Landry."

"You were on the FBI's naughty list, too."

"I was," Brand said with a nod and a faint

whisper of a smile. "Unfairly in my case. What about yours?"

The smile hadn't disappeared, but the room felt instantly colder and less hospitable.

"Definitely unfair in my case," he said firmly. "All the way around, as a matter of fact."

"So we've concluded," Quinn said mildly, waving at the empty chair beside Olivia. "Sit. You must be exhausted."

Landry wished he could make a stand, but his aching legs told him to stop being a stubborn fool. He sank gratefully into the armchair, turning so he could keep both Quinn and Brand in sight.

"We know Darryl Boyle was working with the BRI. We have no reason to think you were, despite your unexplained disappearance. Would you like to explain it?"

Landry glanced at Olivia. "Not at this time."

"Understandable. There's hot food in the kitchen downstairs, and you'd probably like to take advantage of indoor plumbing about now. Sharp can show you where everything is."

"That's it?" Landry asked.

Quinn's sandy eyebrows lifted a notch. "Did you expect something else?"

"You're an ex-spook. I guess I anticipated some sort of enhanced interrogation techniques."

"You've already been through enough of those. Haven't you?" The gentleness of Quinn's tone caught Landry off guard. Apparently, it came as a surprise to Olivia, as well; she stared at her boss with a look of confusion.

"Go get settled. Get warm. Eat some food, drink some water and then get some sleep. We'll all still be here in the morning. Maybe you'll feel more like talking then."

Olivia rose first, heading for the door in stony silence. Landry followed her out, catching up with her halfway to the stairs.

She turned to look at him, her eyes snapping with anger. "That bastard's trying to play you."

Landry nodded. "Yeah, I know. We used to interrogate suspects, too, remember?"

She let out a long, slow breath, visibly trying to relax. "I know. And I know he needs the information. Hell, I still don't know everything that happened to you, either. And I'd like to."

He shook his head. "No, you wouldn't."

She put her hand on his arm, her fingers still icy from the hike in the snow. "I need to know. So when you're ready—"

He covered her hand with his for a moment then gently pulled her hand away, taking a step back from her. "I'm not sure I'll ever be ready, Olivia. Can you deal with that?"

She gazed up at him, her blue eyes troubled. "Can you?"

He nodded toward the stairs. "Quinn said something about food and water?"

She pressed her lips to a thin line. "Yeah. Follow me."

She headed down the hallway toward the staircase, her spine rigid with annoyance. He couldn't hold back a smile at the sight of a pissed-off Olivia Sharp stalking ahead of him like a lioness on the hunt.

He'd missed the hell out of this woman.

OLIVIA WAS FINALLY, blessedly warm. A hot meal, a long, steamy shower and the marvel of central heating had managed to drive away the last of her chills and leave her feeling toasty and half-asleep.

In fact, she must have dozed off for a few moments, for when the soft knock at her dormitory door jarred her awake, the shock left her nerves jangling and her head buzzing.

"Olivia?" Landry spoke quietly from the other side of the door.

She pushed herself to a sitting position on the bed. "Come in."

He slipped inside, stopping just inside the room. "I'm sorry. Did I wake you?"

She resisted the urge to rub her gritty eyes. "No. I'm up. For now."

He walked a few steps closer, flashing a lopsided smile. "Same here. I just wanted to check on you. It was a long hike."

"I'm fine." She patted the edge of the bed. "Sit."

He sat, turning to face her. "I know I gave you a hard time, but thank you for making me come down here. I guess over the past year, I forgot I don't always have to be an army of one."

She'd had to learn the same lesson, she realized. Especially since she'd come to The Gates specifically to investigate a few of her fellow agents suspected of being the source of the devastating information leaks that had put people's lives at risk.

"The people who work here are rough around the edges, but they're good agents. And we really do have each other's back. Quinn wouldn't have it any other way."

"I'm still not sure I like him. I know I don't trust him."

She couldn't blame him for that. "I don't trust him to pick me over the mission. But I trust his passion for protecting this country and its people."

"But you're a security and investigations company. Not a branch of the military."

"And yet, we stand in the breach. There are a lot of people in these hills who just want to live a decent life without fear. And there are a lot of people in these same hills who prey on those good people because they can. Because they're ruthless and better armed."

He flashed her a bemused smile, triggering the dimples that knocked a decade off his age and made her insides twist with desire. "Still protecting and serving, huh? Without all the bureaucratic crap that used to make you nuts."

"It's not all small-scale like trying to take down the BRI. We have some big clients who pay a lot for our training and expertise. It's just—taking down the BRI is Quinn's passion right now."

"Why's that?"

She shrugged, realizing she'd never bothered to ask the question of her wily boss. "I guess maybe it has something to do with his having grown up in these hills. I don't know. Maybe he knows what it's like to be a victim of the predators."

"Or he was a predator himself," Landry murmured. "And maybe he wants to make up for it."

Olivia looked at her former partner through narrowed eyes. She hadn't ever considered the possibility that Quinn had once been one of the human vipers who stalked the Appalachian Mountains. "I don't know. Maybe you're right."

Landry reached across the narrow space between them, taking her hand. "It doesn't matter what inspired him, I guess. We all have mistakes in our pasts we can't correct. At least he's trying to make things better around here instead of worse."

The feel of his rough palm against hers felt right, she realized, dropping her gaze to their joined hands. She'd missed him so intensely over the past two years that having him here, touching him and hearing him speak in that deep Georgia drawl she'd always loved, seemed like a dream she'd wake from any moment.

"Are you really here?" she asked, feeling immediately foolish.

He smiled at her again, making her heart skip a beat. "Feels a little unreal, doesn't it?"

She nodded. "I didn't think I'd ever see you again."

He lifted her hand to his mouth, brushing her knuckles with his lips. "I used to have dreams of you. That you were beside me again. Nothing big. Just beside me, sitting close enough that I could feel the warmth of your body by mine. Hear your breathing. And then I'd wake up." He let go of her hand and dropped his own hands to his knees. "Doesn't matter. Here you are. Warm and breathing."

"Are you never going to tell me what happened to you when you were taken captive?"

"It's not important."

"I can tell it's still important to *you*."

"I'm okay." He flashed another smile, but even the distracting dimples couldn't make it look anything but forced.

But she didn't want to push him. If he needed to talk about what he'd gone through, he'd do it in his own time.

She hoped.

"I don't want to keep you up if you're tired." He started to get up.

She caught his hand, holding him in place. "Don't go."

He looked down at her hand on his. When he spoke, his voice was a low rasp. "Are you sure you want me to stay?"

She knew what he was asking.

"Yes."

He sat in front of her again, closer this time. He turned his hand until it was palm to palm with hers, their fingers twining. "I like your hair short."

She laughed at the non sequitur. "I like yours longer."

He grinned again, the expression deliciously sincere. "Couldn't find many barbershops out in the wilderness."

"That's where you've been all this time?"

"Most of it." He took her other hand, twined his fingers with hers.

"Where did you stay?"

"Camped out a lot. Stayed at cheap roadside motels now and then, when I could spare a little cash."

"How'd you get any cash?" She leaned closer, letting the warmth of his nearness envelop her. "Did you steal?"

"Define *steal*." He grinned at her frown. "I might have eaten a crab apple off someone's tree now and then. But mostly I used money I'd stashed away in case of emergency."

She rubbed the back of his hand with her thumb. "You were expecting an emergency?"

"*Expecting* might be too strong a word. I just anticipated the possibility. And tried to prepare for the worst-case scenario."

"And was what happened the worst case?" She looked up at him.

"Not the worst."

"But bad enough."

He gave her hands a squeeze. "Let it go for now, Livvie. Okay?"

She would have liked to argue, but she didn't want to risk making him get up and leave. "Okay."

"Thank you."

"For now," she added.

He smiled again. "Yeah, I know you don't give up. You're like a bulldog with a chew toy."

"Flattering."

"A beautiful bulldog. A svelte bulldog."

"I think that's an oxymoron."

"Who're you calling an oxymoron?"

She laughed. "I missed this."

"Talking nonsense?"

She stroked his hand again. "Talking nonsense with you."

"Know what I missed?" His voice deepened. Roughened.

Her heartbeat sped up immediately in response. When she spoke, her own voice sounded breathless. "What?"

"This." He leaned forward, closing the space between them, and touched his mouth to hers.

Chapter Ten

When they'd been lovers, there had been passion. Tenderness. Laughter. Even sometimes anger. But never, ever this tentative, questing sensation, like two strangers coming together for a stolen kiss.

Landry drew back and studied her face, trying to read the nuances of each expression flitting across her features as her gaze met his with the same quizzical alertness.

"You're different, aren't you?"

He nodded. "So are you."

"But I still want you." Her raw admission sent a blazing arrow of desire shooting straight to his core. "I just don't know—"

He curled his hand around the back of her neck and gently pulled her into an undemanding embrace, struggling to dial back his body's physical response to her touch. He wanted to reconnect to her, as the friends they'd always been, even if they couldn't be lovers again. Rushing into something they'd regret was a bad idea.

"That feels good," she said as he stroked his hand lightly up and down her spine.

"I don't want to lose you again." He brushed his cheek against her temple, starting to enjoy the exquisite tension of holding her close without any intention of taking things any further. "We were friends first, and I'd like to be friends again."

She lifted her hands, cradling his face between her palms. "I'd like that, too, but—" Her words cut off with a little huff, and she bent toward him, covering his mouth with hers.

There was no hesitation in her kiss. No tentativeness. Just a slow, thorough taking that made his head spin and his heartbeat crank up to hyperspeed. Any thought of differences, of unfamiliarity, were swallowed up by the rising heat between them.

This. He wanted this.

He wanted *her*. Right now, just as she was.

She tugged him down to the bed, parting her thighs to let him settle on top of her. One long leg wrapped around his legs, pinning him to her.

"Don't think," she breathed against his lips.

Threading his fingers through her hair, he deepened the kiss, tasting the minty hint of toothpaste on her tongue. She curled her fingers in his T-shirt and tugged the fabric upward, grumbling when he pulled away from the kiss long enough to whip the shirt over his head.

As he bent to kiss her again, she splayed her fingers against his chest, running them through the coarse hair. She hadn't forgotten how much he liked her hands on him, tracing, teasing, arousing—

A hard rap on the door sent a ripple of raw shock through his nervous system. Olivia growled a soft profanity against his throat and dropped her head back to the pillows.

"What?" she barked toward the closed door.

"Quinn wants to see Landry." Seth's quiet drawl held a touch of amusement, as if he knew exactly what he was interrupting.

"Tell him I'm not his employee, and I'll talk to him in the morning." Landry glanced at Olivia, who was watching him through slightly narrowed eyes. "What?" he added more quietly.

"It's possible he has information you might need," she said in an equally hushed tone.

"It's possible I need a cold shower before I can appear anywhere outside this room," he growled, rolling up to a sitting position and leaning forward in an attempt to get his body back under control.

"I'll go stall Hammond, see if I can find out more about what Quinn wants." She stood and unhurriedly straightened her clothes. Landry watched her smooth the fabric he'd held bunched in his hands mere moments earlier, his heart still pounding a steady cadence of lust.

"Maybe if we hurry—"

Smiling, she bent and kissed him, a slow, wet, deep kiss that made his blood ignite. "Stay put. I'll be back."

As he retrieved his discarded T-shirt, he tried to make out the muted conversation Olivia was having with Seth Hammond outside, but they'd apparently moved too far away from the door. He gave himself a quick once-over and realized she'd managed to unbutton his jeans and get the zipper halfway down without his realizing it. Talented girl!

He zipped up and finger-combed his hair, wishing the dorm rooms in the basement of The Gates had come equipped with a mirror. He didn't need to show up at his command performance with Alexander Quinn looking as if a tall, blonde bombshell had just tried to have her way with him.

Even if she had.

The door opened suddenly and Olivia slipped inside, her expression serious.

"What is it?" he asked.

"An agent has gone missing. Grant Carver. Quinn thinks the BRI have taken him hostage."

A chill washed over Landry, despite the cozy warmth of the room. "When?"

"Sometime this afternoon. His wife called Quinn when he didn't come back from a quick run."

"Couldn't he have just gotten stranded somewhere?"

"That was the assumption. Until she followed his tracks and came upon a patch of snow that looked as if there'd been a struggle. Carver's hat was in the snow. So was an alarming amount of blood. She called the local cops. One of the cops who took the call was Dennison's wife, Sara. She called Dennison to let him know."

Landry sank to the end of the bed, feeling sick. "Any reason why the BRI would go after this guy Carver? Has he had run-ins with any of them?"

Olivia sat next to him, close enough to touch. But he kept his hands on his knees, too wound up to trust himself to touch her. There was a lot about his time in BRI captivity he hadn't told her. Things that he didn't like to think about, things that showed up in his nightmares all too often recently.

"Quinn asked Carver's wife that question. She said no. Some of her distant relatives are involved with the local BRI cell, and she thought that was probably why they could live where they do without too many troubles with the militia members."

"Live where they do?"

She turned to look at him. "They live on the

bottom slope of Fowler Ridge. Near that BRI enclave we hiked through today."

"YOU SAID IT happened this afternoon?" Landry's
tone was neutral, but his expressive eyes gave
away the emotions roiling behind his mask of
calm—anger, worry and guilt Olivia had expected, given the possibility that the mountain
rescue The Gates agents had pulled off earlier
that day might well have led to the BRI's retal-
iatory attack on one of the company's agents.

But the fear that roiled behind his green-eyed
gaze caught her by surprise.

Landry was afraid. And in all the time she'd
known him, she'd rarely seen him afraid of anything.

"If you're wondering if it's connected to you,
we don't know." Quinn spoke in a calm tone that
didn't manage to hide the fact that he believed
Landry's presence in their midst might have pre-
cipitated Carver's abduction.

"You know," Landry growled, "I should get
out of here. All I'm doing is making things that
much harder for you."

Quinn shook his head. "We don't negotiate
with terrorists. We certainly don't hand over innocent people to them to get our agents back.
Carver knew what he signed on for."

"Carver has a wife. A family." Landry glanced
at Olivia.

She'd told him about Carver's pregnant wife and two kids because he'd asked, and she wasn't going to lie to him, even to protect his feelings.

"Nobody has come to us with any demands," Adam Brand said from his seat next to Quinn at the conference table. Besides Landry and herself, there were nine agents seated at the long oak table—Adam Brand and Sutton Calhoun at the head with Quinn, Mark Fitzpatrick, Cain Dennison, Kyle Jackson, Nick Darcy, McKenna Rigsby and Caleb Cooper. All good men in a nasty fight—Brand and Rigsby were former FBI agents, while Calhoun, Dennison, Jackson and Fitzpatrick had all been in the military. Darcy had been with the Diplomatic Security Service for several years, Caleb Cooper had been a narcotics cop in Birmingham, Alabama, and Quinn had been in more dangerous hot spots around the globe than any of them, and he'd lived to tell.

Landry could do a lot worse for backup. But Olivia had a feeling it wasn't the quality of people willing to watch his back that was fueling his fear.

She'd seen the same look in his eyes up on the mountain just before the guys from The Gates had shown up to run off their assailants. It had started when that man from the BRI had spoken.

Had Landry recognized the voice?

"Let's just sit tight for now. The local law is

out looking for Carver. Let's let them do their jobs," Quinn suggested.

"Do you have any idea what kind of things they might do to him?" Landry's voice came out in a strangled growl. Olivia put her hand on his arm but he shrugged away her touch.

Quinn nodded. "We have some idea, yes."

"If he's not leverage—"

"There's a limited amount of information Carver could share with the BRI," Quinn said calmly. "Because of his familial connection to the group, we've kept him away from cases involving the militia group. I'm sure they know that."

"So he *is* leverage."

"Possibly. But there's nothing we can do about it at the moment, so I'd concentrate on something else." Quinn's gaze settled on Landry. "Calhoun says you reacted strongly this afternoon on the mountain, when one of the men who challenged you spoke. You had your back to him, so you must have recognized the voice?"

Landry looked reluctant to speak, but after a moment he nodded. "I think I did."

"Do you know who he was?" Quinn asked.

Olivia could tell from Quinn's tone that he already knew exactly who had accosted them on the mountain earlier that day. He just wanted to establish whether Landry knew.

"I don't know the man's name," Landry answered, looking down at his hands twisting together in his lap. He pulled them apart and gripped the arms of his chair. "I couldn't tell you what he looked like, either. But I'd know that voice in a noisy crowd."

"He was one of your captors?" Olivia asked quietly.

His gaze snapped up to meet hers, full of anger and no small measure of humiliation. "One of them. The worst of them."

"I realize you probably would prefer not to remember what happened during your time in captivity—" Quinn began.

Landry cut him off. "If you're thinking of hooking me up with a shrink or hypnotist or whatever you spook types like to use to poke around in a person's brain, forget it. I don't remember anything that could help you find your missing man. When I got away, I just ran as far and as fast as I could. I'm sure they've already moved operations somewhere else. They moved me around a lot before I got away, so I don't think they have a permanent base for their snatch-and-grab operations."

"Fair enough. Meeting adjourned." Quinn stood, the look he gave the other men sitting around the table serving as a silent warning— Cade Landry was off-limits, for the time being, anyway.

Olivia could tell most of the other agents

weren't happy about their boss playing softball with Landry, but they knew better than to voice their dissent at the conference table. They could take it up with him privately later—and from the displeasure in their expressions, Olivia was pretty sure that at least two or three of them would.

But for now, she and Landry were free to go.

"I need to get out of here," Landry murmured as he caught up with her down the hall. "I should never have tried to play this straight. Those bastards don't know the meaning of playing it straight."

She caught his arm as he started toward the stairs. "You're not leaving."

"I'm not staying."

"You know what the conditions out there are like. It's only going to get colder now that the sun has set."

"How cold do you think Grant Carver is right now?" His voice lowered to a deep growl. "Do you have a clue what they might be doing to him?"

"Yes," she answered tightly. "I do have an idea. Maybe you should go compare notes with one of our agents, Hunter Bragg. The BRI took him hostage last year. He has the scars to prove it."

Landry looked away from her, his expression queasy. "They're relentless. They're not really any good at interrogations. They don't know how to play the game, how to get any real information. They just do it because they're sadistic bastards who get off on the feeling of power it gives them to make a grown man scream." He tugged his arm away from her grasp and started down the stairs.

She ran down the steps after him, tripping in her hurry to keep up. He caught her before she tumbled, pulling her tightly against him. A jolt of pure animal awareness bolted through her from the point where her hips met his, and she dug her fingers into the muscles of his upper arms.

"Don't go," she whispered.

"I can't stay."

"You can. At least tonight. Stay tonight."

He looked away from her, his gaze scanning the room before it returned to lock with hers. "You know we can't pick up where we left off."

"You mean you don't want to."

For a second his expression softened, and he looked like the man she used to know, the man who had loved her and made her as happy as she could ever remember being.

"You know I do."

"Then stay. We don't have to pick up where we left off, but please, don't go away again. Not yet, not while you're in trouble. Let me help you."

He brushed her hair back from her cheek, his touch so impossibly tender it made tears sting her eyes. She blinked them back, not willing to let them fall. "I don't know if you can. I don't know if it's fixable."

"Then you can just get some rest. Most of the guys will be up all night trying to piece together what happened to Carver and how we proceed at daylight. We should get some sleep so we can spell them in the morning."

"We?" He tugged lightly at her hair.

"You used to be a damn good FBI agent. I don't think you've forgotten everything you learned at the academy, have you?"

"Trying to bend me to your will by dangling a mystery in front of me?"

"Is it working?"

"Maybe." He bent toward her until his forehead touched hers. "You win. I'll stay. For now."

She gave his arms a squeeze. "Come on. Let's get some sleep. Tomorrow's going to be a long day."

He didn't resist as she led him back down to the basement dormitory rooms, stopping outside the door of her room. "As tempting as it is to go back in there with you…"

She smiled. "The goal is sleep?"

He nodded toward the room across from hers, where he'd stashed his own things. "I'll be there in the morning. I promise."

She pressed her hand to the front of his shirt, feeling the reassuring thud of his heartbeat against her palm. "If you aren't, I'm hunting you down."

He sneaked a quick look around, as if reassuring himself they were alone, then bent and gave her a quick kiss. "Get some sleep."

She waited in her doorway until he entered his own room and closed the door behind him, then turned and entered her own dorm room, flicking on the light.

The bed was the way she'd left it, slightly rumpled and full of recent memories of Landry— the way he smelled, the sensation of his hands on her bare skin, the electric thrill of their bodies pressed close and straining for more. She closed her eyes and sank on the edge of the bed, swamped by memories. Of their first meeting, the literal electric shock that passed between them as they shook hands, making them laugh and snatch their hands away.

The more visceral shock of desire the first time they'd taken a step past the slow burn of attraction and kissed at the end of a long day at work.

She lay back on the bed, opening her eyes to stare at the ceiling. They hadn't planned to start a relationship. For weeks, even months, they pretended what was happening between them was just chemical. Two people enjoying each other, no strings attached.

But there had been strings. Probably from the

beginning. Despite her tumultuous childhood with a promiscuous and reckless mother, despite his parents' distant, businesslike marriage, somehow, they'd been foolish enough to believe in the possibility of forever.

And then the bombing at the warehouse in Richmond had blown everything apart.

The tears she'd been fighting earlier leaked from her eyes and slid down her cheeks. She brushed them away, angry at the sign of weakness and glad that Landry wasn't here to see it.

She couldn't start thinking about forever again. She just had to focus on getting through one day at a time. She had to figure out a way to get Landry out of the mess he was in. Give him back the life that the BRI had stolen from him when he'd ended up their captive.

Then maybe she'd figure out how to say a proper goodbye this time.

HE'D ARRIVED AT his apartment after midnight, the metallic taste of fear in his mouth and his mind reeling with questions he didn't know how to answer. He'd tried to help Agent Rigsby, hadn't he? It had been a risk to try to call her and warn her that someone else from the FBI was coming after her.

But before he'd hung up the phone with Darryl Boyle, supervisory special agent with the FBI's

Knoxville field office, he'd known McKenna Rigsby was in big trouble.

Boyle was railroading her. The man had said nothing incriminating, but Landry had heard the flicker of eagerness in his voice when he told Landry Rigsby had called him, as well.

He was going after her. And he had no intention of bringing her back alive.

Landry had tried to help her, but he couldn't reach her before Boyle did. He wasn't even sure where she'd be—she'd set a trap, hoping to ensnare the person who had tried to kill her before, and she might not have been in either of the two locations where she'd told him and Boyle she'd be.

He'd just hoped she'd got away. He'd done all he dared. He had his own trouble with the FBI, with a career that was already on life support. He couldn't risk sticking his neck out, in case he was wrong about Boyle.

What a coward he'd been.

When the four men materialized out of the shadows of his living room, he'd been unprepared for a fight. They took him down with ease, binding him with duct tape and hustling him out to a van he hadn't noticed parked outside his unit.

That had been the beginning of his trip to hell.

Chapter Eleven

Olivia woke to darkness and a gnawing sense of unease she couldn't place. She knew she was in one of the dorm rooms in the basement of the old Buckley Mansion that Alexander Quinn had transformed into The Gates. She hadn't been awakened by a sudden noise or an unexpected touch in the night. She'd just gone from sleep to animal awareness in one fluid motion, without any idea why all of her senses were suddenly tingling.

She listened to the darkness, waiting for some noise, some sensation to remind her what had summoned her from sleep, but there was nothing but the languid silence of a mostly unoccupied space. Down here, in the rooms built out of the mansion's stone foundation, even the creaks and groans of the old house settling rarely penetrated this quiet sanctuary.

Maybe one of the other agents had come down to catch some sleep before morning, she thought, pushing off the covers and swinging her feet down to the cold floor. Shivering, she felt around for the slip-on shoes she'd retrieved from her desk in the agents' bull pen and slid them on her feet.

She padded to the door, stopping to listen before she opened it and stepped outside into the dimly lit main room. The basement dormitory consisted of one long, wide corridor with six small bedrooms branching off on either side, three to the right and three to the left. There was a large bathroom at the end of the hall. That door was open, as were four of the other doors in the dorm.

Only Landry's door remained closed. Apparently, all of the other agents remaining on the premises were still upstairs with Quinn.

She crossed the hallway and pressed her ear to the closed door, wondering if she'd heard noises coming from the room across the hall. But she could hear nothing from inside, except a faint creaking noise that might have been the bedsprings shifting under Landry's weight.

Or was she simply imagining that she could hear sounds of occupation, because the alternative—the possibility that what had jarred her awake had been Landry sneaking out of the dorm—was something she didn't want to believe?

Just open the door, her anxiety whispered in

her ear. *Open it and you'll know if he bugged out on you.*

She turned the door handle, half expecting it to be locked. But it moved easily in her grasp, the door swinging quietly inward.

Landry was there, still in the bed. The creaking noise she'd heard repeated twice, louder now.

He was moving in his sleep, jerky twitches rather than thrashing that might hint at a violent nightmare. But the light angling through the open doorway fell on his face, revealing an expression that was nothing short of terror.

Landry jerked up to a sitting position so suddenly, she couldn't hold back a gasp of surprise. Her hand flexed, rattling the doorknob, and his gaze whipped up to meet hers.

"I'm sorry," she breathed. "I didn't mean—"

He pulled his knees up under the twisted sheets and rested his elbows on them, pressing his face into his hands for a long moment. The muscles in his back flexed, revealing pale streaks she hadn't seen before.

She reached for the switch on the wall and flooded the room with light.

Landry squinted up at her. "What the hell?"

"What are those?" she asked, crossing to the bed to get a better look at the pale scars marring his back. "Oh, my God. What happened to you?"

He looked away from her. "The Blue Ridge Infantry happened."

She touched one of the pale scars. He flinched and she pulled her hand back quickly. "They beat you."

"You didn't think it was a trip to the beach, did you?"

"What did they hit you with?" She tried to school her expression, to approach the question without emotion. She'd seen terrible things as an FBI agent and also working at The Gates. She'd seen some of the worst things people could do to their fellow human beings, and she'd always thought herself to be stoic and controlled.

But the thought of someone wielding a whip or a stick or whatever had made these scars—

"They're healed. They don't matter." He reached over and picked up his discarded T-shirt, pulling it over his head. "You should be trying to get some sleep."

"I was. Something woke me."

He frowned. "You think you heard something?"

"I'm not sure." She sank onto the side of his bed. "I guess maybe I'm still on edge."

"I can't imagine why," he murmured in a dry tone.

She managed a smile. "Are you sure you're okay? You were tossing and turning when I came in."

"Unfamiliar bed."

"Yeah." She plucked at the bedsheets. "You

haven't really had a chance to talk to anybody about what the BRI put you through, have you?"

"Couldn't exactly go into therapy while I was running for my life."

"You know it's not healthy to try to bury a traumatic experience."

He laughed softly. "I seem to remember a beautiful, hardheaded FBI agent who chafed at the idea of post-operation counseling."

"And that same agent didn't cope very well after Richmond, remember? I lost so much after what happened at the warehouse. I lost myself." She blinked back the rush of hot tears burning her eyes. "I lost you."

He looked up at her, his green eyes glistening with pain. "You really think post-trauma counseling would have saved us?"

"I don't know." She shook her head, feeling suddenly helpless. "I just wish we'd fought harder. I wish we'd valued our relationship more."

"You think I threw it away, don't you?" His lips thinned to a hard line. "You think I pushed you away."

"I used to." She rubbed away a tear that trickled from the corner of her eye. "But I pushed you away, too. I knew you were angry with me. I should have worked harder to be certain I understood why. Maybe if I'd tried, you'd have confronted me after what the debriefing team told you about my statement, and I could have assured you they were lying."

"I'm not sure I'd have believed you," he admitted, looking away.

"I'd have made you believe me."

"You shouldn't have had to make me believe you. I should have believed you because of who you were. What you were to me."

His use of the past tense made her stomach ache. "You never could. Could you?"

The sadness in his eyes hurt her heart. "I wanted to." He shook his head. "I guess I was so used to lies spoken as casually as small talk. There were so many things I wanted desperately as a kid to believe. Promises my parents made that they never kept." He laughed bleakly. "You'd think all those years later, I could have just let it go. They never really wanted kids, and when they had one by accident, they figured out a way to go on with their lives as if I had never happened. It had nothing to do with me. Not really. I didn't matter enough for it to be about me."

Growing up poor with a flighty, promiscuous mother, Olivia had pictured the lives of wealthy people as a utopian promised land, where every child had two parents, all they wanted to eat, all the clothes they wanted to wear and every luxury she could imagine.

She'd never realized there were privations

that money couldn't alleviate, until she'd met Cade Landry.

"I guess you haven't spoken with your parents since you went missing?" she asked.

"I don't imagine they care."

She shook her head. His parents had done one hell of a number on him with their casual, thoughtless neglect. "What about Mary? Does she know you're still alive?"

He shook his head. "Mary's safer thinking I'm dead."

"You don't think the BRI's reach goes all the way to Savannah, do you?"

"No point in risking it." He shrugged. "Mary's got a new batch of kids to raise. Did you know that? Last time I talked to her, she was working for a lawyer and his wife. Seem like nice people, from what she said. And the kids are stinking cute. She emailed me photos from Christmas a year ago."

His nanny, Mary Allen, had been the closest thing he'd had to a parent growing up. She'd been only twenty years old when his parents had hired her, shortly after Landry's birth, and she'd given him the attention his parents had withheld.

But even she had kept a certain distance, emotionally. Or tried to, Olivia supposed, thinking of a few things Landry had let slip about his relationship with his nanny. Mary had seemed determined to give Landry's parents every chance to be what he needed them to be. She hadn't wanted him to replace his parents with her.

Olivia had met Mary once, on a weekend trip to Savannah early in her relationship with Landry. She'd been a trim, pretty woman with curly brown hair liberally streaked with gray and kind blue eyes that had made Olivia instantly wish she'd had a Mary Allen in her own life growing up.

"I've had a lot of time to think. To navel-gaze, I think was how you used to put it." Landry slanted a lopsided smile at her. "I do wish you'd come to me and told me the truth. I don't know if I'd have believed you right away, but in time, I think I would have."

An ache of regret throbbed in her chest. "You think so, do you?"

"You probably wouldn't have forgiven me for doubting you, so I'm not sure it would have solved anything," he admitted. "But it would have been comforting anyway. Knowing you didn't think I was lying about the order to go into the warehouse."

She turned to face him, catching his hands in hers. "I never once believed you were lying about that. Not once. No matter what other trust issues I had, I never doubted you were a good FBI agent. You didn't ignore orders on a whim, and you didn't put people's lives in danger for selfish reasons. I know you wanted to stop those guys. I did, too. But I wouldn't have defied orders and blundered into that warehouse just because I was eager to make an arrest. And neither would you."

His eyes narrowed briefly. "You mean that, don't you?"

"I do."

He blinked rapidly, and she didn't miss the hint of moisture in his eyes as he looked down at their clasped hands. "Thank you."

"I know a lot has happened since Richmond. I know we can't go back to what we had then. I don't really want to."

He let go of her hands. "Yeah, a whole lot of water under that bridge."

She took his hands again, giving them a sharp tug to make him look at her. "It wasn't enough then. Not for either one of us. It's not something we should aspire to now."

His eyes narrowed. "Aspire to?"

"I don't want to live this way anymore. I want more than half a relationship. I want to be able to trust someone else. I want someone else to be able to trust me, too."

He nodded. "I get that."

"Maybe that person will never be you. That's something you're going to have to figure out. I just know that as much as I loved you then, it wasn't enough. It would never have been enough, not the way it was. Not with everything we held back."

He released a huff of air. "Yeah. You're right. It wouldn't have been."

She let his hands go and stood up. "I'm going back to my room now. You try to get some sleep. And if you need me, you know where to find me."

It took strength to walk out of his room and not look back, but she made herself do it. Made herself walk across the wide corridor, enter her dorm room and close the door behind her.

And if she cried herself to sleep, it was nobody's business but her own.

"WE STOCKED UP for the snowstorm," Mark Fitzpatrick told Landry as he passed him a plate of eggs, bacon and toast, steaming hot from the stove.

"Did you buy up all the milk and bread?" Landry asked with a smile, knowing that a fellow Southerner would get the joke.

"What was left." Fitz grinned. "Don't you wonder why people don't make a run on charcoal and grills instead when snow is forecast? Seems those things would be more useful."

Landry joined the other agents who'd gathered at the conference table for breakfast. Their numbers had expanded, he noted. There was a small, dark-haired woman sitting next to Sutton

Calhoun, and across from her, a taller brunette had joined Adam Brand and Alexander Quinn, her head close to theirs in conversation.

"Ivy Calhoun and Delilah Brand," Olivia told him as he settled beside her at the table. "They're both cops in Bitterwood. They worked the overnight shift as part of the department's snow contingency plan or something."

"And there's another guy's wife who's a cop, too, right? You said she was called out on Grant Carver's disappearance?"

"Right. Sara Dennison. Dennison headed out last night to meet up with her and see if she could tell us any more about the investigation. I guess they haven't made it back here yet."

Two more people came into the conference room, still dressed in heavy clothing and red-cheeked from the cold outside. One was a tall, rawboned man in his midthirties with wavy brown hair and dark eyes, while the woman beside him was petite, blonde and sweet-faced. They both gave Landry a curious glance.

Then the man did a double take. "Cade Landry."

Landry sighed. He'd spent the past few months trying to look as different from his FBI photo as he could, but apparently there were some things a man couldn't change about himself.

"Landry, this is Anson Daughtry, our IT director, and his wife, Ginny, one of our accountants." Olivia gave Anson and Ginny a pointed look. "Who're both supposed to be somewhere sunny on their honeymoon."

"And miss the fun? Who do you think we are?" Daughtry set down their plates of food and pulled out a chair for his wife before settling across from Landry and Olivia. "We just walked in—anything new on Carver?"

"Not that we've heard," Olivia answered.

Daughtry gave Landry a curious look. "I heard you'd shown up, but I thought you two were stuck in your cabin."

"You knew I was at her cabin?"

"He was the one I had monitoring that bank account in Barrowville," Olivia murmured.

"I see." He arched an eyebrow at Daughtry. "And from that, you figured out who I was and where I was?"

"Well, we knew you had once had a relationship with Bombshell Barb—" Daughtry's mouth snapped shut, and Landry saw Ginny dig an elbow into her husband's ribs. "We knew you were once involved with Agent Sharp, so when the bank activity showed up—"

Landry lowered his voice. "Your boss likes to stay on top of what's going on in all his agents' lives, doesn't he?"

Daughtry rolled his eyes. "You have no idea, man."

At the head of the table, Quinn's cell phone

trilled. He answered it with a brief "Hello" and just listened for a moment. "Okay, thanks."

The room had grown quiet, all eyes turned to their boss.

"That was Dennison. A call came in to Sara's radio while they were checking in on his grand-mother. Patrol officers just got a call about a body found in the snow about a mile south of Fowler Ridge."

Brand was the first to ask the obvious ques-tion. "Carver?"

"We're not sure. Dennison's heading over there with Sara to take a look." Quinn's gaze landed on Mark Fitzpatrick. "You know Carver's wife pretty well, don't you?"

Fitz nodded. "Lexie and I went to high school with her. You want me to go wait with her in case we get bad news?"

Pressure built inside Landry's chest and swelled upward, making his head pound. He had to get out of this room, out of this building.

He had to get as far away from these people as he could, before anyone else got hurt.

He was on his feet and halfway out the door before anyone else reacted. He heard Quinn call his name, heard the scrape of chair legs on the floor as he swept through the door and down the hall.

Footsteps padded after him, hurrying to catch

up as he reached the stairs. Olivia's voice rang out behind him. "This is not your fault."

He turned swiftly to look at her. "You're trying to tell me you honestly think the BRI would have taken your colleague if I hadn't shown up at your cabin two days ago like a stupid fool?" He felt sick, the half a plate of bacon and eggs he'd eaten heavy in his gut. "I knew there was a risk. I knew it. I just thought I would be the only one who would suffer if it all went wrong. I should have known better."

"You don't know this had anything to do with you."

"Of course I do. That man on the mountain—he knew exactly who I was! I could tell from the tone of his voice."

"Just because you recognized his voice doesn't mean he recognized you."

"Then why, after all this time of your friend Carver living safely on that mountain, did he get grabbed the very same day that bastard ran into us on the mountain? Can you answer me that?" Agitation rose like bile in his throat, spurring him into motion again. He started down the stairs at a reckless pace, two steps at a time, and bolted toward the front door.

Olivia raced down after him, grabbing him as he reached for the handle. "Damn it, no! Don't you dare walk out on me again! Not like this."

"It could have been you, Livvie." He turned

to look at her, his heart contracting at the concern that darkened her blue eyes. "You could be that body they found in the snow. I never should have come here. I never should have brought this nightmare to your doorstep."

"It's not Carver." Alexander Quinn's voice rang in the foyer, making them both turn to look at him. He walked unhurriedly down the stairs toward them, coming to a stop a few feet away.

"Dennison called back?" Olivia asked, sounding relieved.

"Yes. Halfway to the site, they got a call from the patrolman on the scene. The body had ID on it. Driver's license. Some professional credentials."

Beside Landry, Olivia frowned. "Professional credentials?"

Quinn walked closer, his gaze sliding from Olivia's face to Landry's. "To be specific, FBI credentials. Someone you both know, actually."

Olivia exchanged a glance with Landry before she looked at her boss again. "Are you telling us—"

"After all this time, Darryl Boyle finally turned up," Quinn said.

Chapter Twelve

"I thought we'd never find Boyle's body. I figured he was somewhere down a hole in the mountains where nobody but the bears would find him." McKenna Rigsby looked up at Nick Darcy, carrying out a whole silent conversation in that one glance.

Olivia had been tangentially involved in the ruse Rigsby and Darcy had set up to trap Darryl Boyle, an FBI agent who'd stupidly tried to co-opt the Blue Ridge Infantry to create a domestic terror act devastating enough to make the government finally start rooting out radicals from within the US borders. But Boyle had turned the tables on Rigsby, and if she and Darcy hadn't been able to convince the head of the Blue Ridge Infantry that Boyle wasn't the ally he made himself out to be, it might have been Rigsby lying dead in the snow rather than Boyle.

"I wonder how long he's been out there," Darcy murmured, looking troubled. Olivia knew he had never fully made peace with trading Boyle's life for Rigsby's, no matter how much he loved her. Like the rest of The Gates agents, he didn't like leaving anyone behind, even someone who'd gone into league with the bad guys.

"Not long." Quinn walked into the conference room, sliding his phone back into his pocket. "Sara said the body was pretty fresh."

"He disappeared months ago," Landry said.

"I know." Quinn glanced at Landry. "There were signs that Boyle had taken more than one beating during the time he's been missing."

Landry's face went pale, and he looked down at his hands clasped tightly together on the table.

Olivia quelled the urge to touch him, knowing he'd just shrug her hand away. But she needed to get him somewhere alone, soon, and see if she could get him to talk about what he'd been through. Whatever the BRI had done to him— and she couldn't imagine they'd been kind in any way—he was still suffering the emotional aftermath.

Repressing that trauma wasn't going to make it go away. And anything he could remember about his time in captivity with the BRI might be important in their quest to take down the vicious militia group.

Quinn crossed until he was standing close to Landry. He waited for Landry to look up before speaking again. "You realize the discovery of

Boyle's body after all this time is only going to reenergize the FBI's investigation into what happened last spring."

Landry gave a solemn nod. "I know. I should get out of here before the FBI comes knocking on your front door."

"I didn't say that." Quinn bent and planted his palms on the table. "But we need to consider what to do with you while the FBI is sniffing around."

"Maybe it's time to turn myself in."

"No." Olivia closed her fingers over his arm. "The last time you tried turning yourself in, the BRI took you captive."

"But I was alone then." He squeezed her hand. "Now I'm not."

Warmth flooded her. "No, you're not."

"I don't think we've reached that point yet," Quinn said. "We're pretty sure there are still people left in the FBI who are sympathetic to the Blue Ridge Infantry."

"Darryl Boyle made that pretty clear. We just don't know who or how many." McKenna Rigsby looked across the table at Landry. "I'm sorry, Landry. I feel as if I'm the reason you went through what you did, because you were trying to help me."

He shook his head quickly. "Don't. You were a target, too. You had every right to try to figure out who in the FBI was trying to kill you.

I'm sorry I didn't work all that out before things went so wrong. I should have been paying better attention." His gaze dropped and he tugged his arm away from Olivia's grip. "I should have been a better agent."

"You can flog yourself later," Quinn said in a dust-dry tone. "Right now I need you to concentrate on what you might know about the people who took Carver captive. I don't want to lose an agent. We've been damned lucky so far, and I'd like the record to hold."

Landry nodded but didn't say anything more.

"I think we're safe from the FBI until the roads clear, but once they do, we're going to be racing the clock." Quinn looked at the agents surrounding him. "I'd like to stash Landry somewhere the FBI wouldn't think to look for him, but I'm not sure at this point that our established safe houses are a good option. They're too easy to connect to The Gates. Any other suggestions?"

"Rachel's uncle and aunt live over in Bryson City," Seth Hammond suggested. "They've got a guesthouse out back of their place. Rachel and I have stayed there a few times. Nobody'd think to look for Landry there."

"Rachel's his wife," Olivia murmured to Landry.

"A decent option. Any other suggestions?"

"I have family in Alabama who are damned good in a fight," Caleb Cooper said.

"I've considered that option, but I don't want Landry that many hours away."

"What difference does that make?" Olivia asked, not liking the dark gleam she saw in Quinn's eyes.

Her boss glanced at her briefly before turning his pointed gaze to Landry. "Because sooner or later, I believe Mr. Landry will understand the vital need for him to tell us everything he remembers about his time in BRI captivity. And when he does, I don't want to have to drive six hours to hear him out."

Next to Olivia, Landry looked down at the table, his jaw tight with anger. She put her hand on his leg under the table and felt his muscles twitch. "Why don't we start with Bryson City?" she suggested. "As soon as the roads are cleared for travel, I'll drive him there. We'll play tourists for a few days until the FBI gets tired of sniffing around here."

Quinn's gaze remained on Landry's lowered head. "Very well. The temperature is supposed to rise above freezing this afternoon, with enough sunshine to give us a decent melt-off. The roads could be clear enough to drive by morning."

Olivia squeezed Landry's leg. "Then we'll head out first thing in the morning."

"THE HUNTERS ARE nice people." Olivia had spent most of the past hour folding the clothes for their trip to Bryson City. She kept a couple of changes of clothing at the office for emergency situations, she'd explained to Landry when she'd pulled the small overnight bag out of her locker in the agents' bull pen. Added to the clothes they'd brought with them on the hike over the mountain, she had enough to wear for four days. If they could find a laundry in Bryson City, they could stay longer if necessary.

But Landry knew it wouldn't be necessary.

He'd put off facing everything that had happened to him in BRI captivity for long enough.

He caught Olivia's wrist as she placed a pair of socks in one of the suitcases Quinn had provided. "We don't have to go to Bryson City."

She frowned. "You want to go somewhere else?"

"I can tell Quinn everything he needs to know tonight. Get it over with and get out of here so you and everybody else can get on with your lives."

The look on her face nearly unraveled his resolve. "You want to leave? Now? After—" Her lips snapped to a thin line and she turned away.

"It would be better for you, Livvie. Surely you can see that. Even if we can somehow prove I'm not a traitor, there's no way the FBI lets me come back. I'm done there. And I'm not sure what other sort of job I can get that's going to be worth anything. I don't know how to be anything else."

"Quinn would hire you."

"No, he wouldn't. I'm too big a risk. He knows that. So do you."

"Because you worked with the Blue Ridge Infantry? Obviously, you were trying to bring them down." Her brow furrowed. "Right?"

She was trying so hard not to have doubts, but she couldn't quite pull it off. He couldn't really blame her. He hadn't exactly given her a reason to believe in him anymore.

"I was. But I wasn't doing it for the FBI or any other organization that could back me up. I have only my word that I was on the side of the angels, and Quinn can't trust my word." He touched her face, letting his fingers slide lightly over the perfect curve of her cheek. "You can't, either, can you?"

Her jaw tightened, her chin lifting. "I believe you."

"Without any proof?"

Her gaze leveled with his, her eyes a cool, crystalline blue that should have chilled him but warmed him to his core instead. "Your word is the proof. I believe you."

She almost convinced him she did.

She released a soft sigh, as if she could read his own doubts. "Let's just go through with the plan, okay? We'll go to Bryson City to stay for a few days. Once we're there, if you want to tell me everything you can remember about your time in captivity, great. If you feel you need to wait a little longer, that's fine, too. I know you'll do the right thing for Grant Carver."

Landry couldn't stop a soft laugh. "Oh, Livvie. Still twisting the knife with a smile, aren't you?"

She arched an eyebrow at him. "Me?"

"I will do everything I can to help find Carver." God knew, the guilt was starting to eat him up.

"I know you will."

Alexander Quinn stopped by the dorm room a few minutes later. "The roads into North Carolina have been deemed passable by the Tennessee and North Carolina Highway Patrols." He handed over a key to Olivia. "There's a Chevy Tahoe parked out back, gassed up and ready to go. It should be able to handle any icy patches left on the road."

Olivia glanced at Landry. "Is Rachel's uncle expecting us?"

"Yes. He's setting up the guesthouse for you. If anyone asks, you're distant relatives from Georgia, up here to enjoy the winter season in the Smokies."

"I don't want to put anyone else in danger," Landry said. The closer he got to leaving The Gates, the more he feared he was making a mistake. "Maybe I should just wait here for the FBI to show up and take me into custody. I can call a lawyer I know in Richmond, make sure he makes noise with the Richmond field office so they'll know someone's watching."

"Why didn't you do that when you got away from the BRI?" Quinn asked.

He wasn't sure he had a good answer. At the time he got away from his captors, his only thought was to get clear of their reach and find a place to hunker down until he could figure out what to do next.

The problem was, he never really figured out what to do next.

"Go to Bryson City. Do some thinking without the pressure of the FBI breathing down your neck," Quinn suggested. "Maybe you'll figure out how you want to handle things with the FBI from a place of clarity."

Clarity, Landry thought. He wasn't sure he knew what the word meant anymore.

THE DRIVE TO Bryson City took two hours on slick roads through the Smoky Mountains, but the Chevy handled the conditions as well as Olivia could have hoped, and the scenery was so breathtaking she had to struggle to keep her eyes on the road instead of the snowy landscape.

"I wish this was a pleasure trip," Landry murmured as they rounded a curve and came upon another breathtaking mountain vista.

"So do I."

"Do you know anything about this place where we'll be staying?"

"It's actually an extension of a restaurant and music venue, Song Valley Music Hall."

"A music hall?"

She glanced at him, taking in his confusion. "It belongs to Rafe Hunter, Rachel Hammond's uncle."

"Wife of the con man."

"Former con man."

"Whatever."

"Her aunt and uncle have run this place for years. They're actually quite well-known for what they do. Apparently, Rafe Hunter is known in music circles as a brilliant judge of talent. Seth says playing at the Song Valley Music Hall is a badge of honor for a new artist."

Landry was silent for a moment while Olivia eased the Tahoe into a slushy curve. Once they'd reached the straightaway, he added, "Does this Rafe Hunter know who we are and why we're there?"

"He knows I work with Seth. He thinks you're my boyfriend and this is a winter getaway for us." She glanced at Landry and saw him frowning. "Is that a problem? It seemed like the easiest cover story."

"No, it's fine."

"We aren't going to see much of Mr. Hunter, so you don't have to pretend anything."

"That's not the problem, believe me."

"Then what?"

"Are we going to share a room?"

She slanted another look at him and found his intense green gaze on her. Heat flitted up her neck and into her cheeks, and she forced her gaze back to the winding road. "It's a guesthouse. There are two bedrooms."

His voice dropped to a soft growl. "That didn't entirely answer my question."

Her breath caught. "I don't know," she admitted.

"Then maybe that's the answer." He leaned back against his seat. "I think we should both be really sure about anything that happens between us this time. We both ignored a lot of doubts the last time and jumped into things recklessly."

"That's how you remember our relationship?" She tried to quell the sense of hurt that rose in her chest, but she didn't have much luck. "As a reckless mistake?"

"I didn't say that."

"I think you did."

He fell silent for the rest of the drive, tension stretching between them until Olivia felt that she'd snap in two. The sight of the Song Valley Music Hall through the front windshield of the Tahoe was a palpable relief.

The place was packed, parking hard to come by, but Olivia found a slot for the Tahoe near the far end of the parking lot and cut the engine. "You stay here. I'll go find Rafe and tell him we're here."

"Where's the guesthouse?" he asked, giving the low-slung saloon-style facade of the music hall a skeptical look.

"I'm not sure," she admitted. She'd assumed there would be some sort of residential structure attached to the building, but there was nothing like that in sight as she crossed the gravel parking lot and entered the music hall.

An early dinner crowd filled the place with talk and laughter that rang in her ears after the long, mostly silent drive through the mountains. The smiling man at the bar at the back answered her query by pointing to a short, jovial man talking to customers at a nearby table.

Olivia waited for him to finish the conversation, stepping into his path as he turned toward the next table. "Mr. Hunter?"

He had to look up to meet her gaze. His smile widened. "Lord, you must be Olivia. Seth described you over the phone." The twinkle in Rafe Hunter's eye made her wonder if the nickname "Bombshell Barbie" had come up. She tried not to take it as anything but a compliment, but she tired of everyone focusing on the fact that she was tall, blonde and on the curvy side. She was also smart, resourceful and dangerous.

Then again, being underestimated could often work in her favor.

"How far is the guesthouse from here?" she asked as she followed him to a back room in the music hall. The cramped little space was clearly his office; he dug through the lap drawer of the desk and retrieved a key.

"Not far," he said with a smile, nodding for her to follow him back to the main hall, where a four-piece bluegrass band was warming up for their first set. Rafe motioned for her to wait a moment while he crossed to speak with the mandolin player. They exchanged a few words and laughter before Rafe returned to Olivia. "Sorry about that—new act, and there's a record-label scout in the audience tonight. They're as nervous as pigs at a barbecue joint." Rafe laughed at his own joke. "I like to put 'em at ease. They play better if they're laughing."

They stepped out into the chilly twilight air. Overhead, stars and a waxing moon glowed through wisps of clouds visible above the trees. "Y'all get a lot of snow over there in Tennessee?" he asked conversationally as they walked toward the side of the music hall, not far from where she'd parked the Tahoe.

"Enough," she answered, his friendly mountain twang coaxing her own Sand Mountain drawl out to play.

He led her around the building and waved his hand at what the music hall's bright facade had hidden. About twenty yards behind the music hall stood a lovely two-story wood cabin, glowing with warm light from within. "That's where my wife, Janeane, and I live. And right behind that house is the guesthouse. We built it for Janeane's mama, thinking she'd come live with us after Janeane's daddy died. But Donna fell in love with the funeral director and eloped about four weeks later." Rafe laughed, apparently finding the story hilarious.

"That was fast," Olivia commented.

"Well, that's Donna. Fast and brash. It's a big part of her charm." Rafe stopped walking and turned to her, handing her the key he'd brought with them. "Just head on down the flagstone walk past the house and you'll see the place. Janeane knows you're arriving, but be sure to pop your head in the back door and let her know you're here so she won't go for her shotgun." He walked back toward the music hall, laughing.

Olivia started for the Tahoe, but Landry met her halfway, carrying their suitcases in both hands, the shoulder strap of the duffel bag full of their supplies draped across his body.

She relieved him of one of the suitcases. "That was Rafe Hunter."

"I figured." He looked past her at the wood cabin. "Is that it?"

"No, that's Mr. Hunter's place. He said the guesthouse is behind their house, down this flagstone path." Nodding for him to follow, she walked down the dark path, animal awareness prickling the hairs at the back of her neck. How much of her unease could be attributed to the danger lurking around them and how much to the prospect of several days alone with Cade Landry in a scenic mountain cabin, she couldn't say.

The guesthouse came into view as they passed the back corner of the Hunters' cabin, a small, pretty one-story cabin decorated with the slow-melting remains of the earlier snowstorm. Box-wood shrubs flanked the steps up to the porch, giving the log cabin the appearance of a quaint country cottage.

"Cute," Landry commented.

Olivia slanted a look at him.

He met her gaze, smiling. But his smile faded in an instant, and his eyes widened as he looked at something behind her.

She heard the unmistakable clatter of the fore-end of a pump-action shotgun sliding back, ready to fire.

"State your business." The voice behind them was female, mountain-accented and deadly.

Dropping the suitcase to the ground beside her, Olivia lifted her hands and slowly turned to face the small, silver-haired woman pointing a shotgun at her chest.

Swallowing the instant flood of terror that came with facing a shotgun barrel, Olivia forced her voice through her tightened throat. "Janeane Hunter, I presume?"

Chapter Thirteen

"I told her to poke her head in the back door and tell you she'd arrived." What Landry assumed was Rafe Hunter's plaintive voice was audible over the phone Janeane Hunter held to one ear. The shotgun remained in her other hand, though she'd dropped the barrel until it pointed toward their legs instead of their midsections. Landry wondered if they could make a run for it before Janeane Hunter could whip the barrel up and give the fore-end a pump. After another look at her sharp-eyed gaze, he decided it would be folly to try.

Janeane made a face at the phone. "That might've got her shot for sure, you old fool."

"I would have knocked," Olivia offered helpfully.

Janeane flashed her a pointed look, and Olivia pressed her mouth to a thin line. Landry quelled the urge to laugh, despite the jittery adrenaline flooding his system.

"Did she show you any ID?" Janeane asked.

"No, but hell, she looked like what Seth described, and there can't be too many that do," Rafe said. Landry couldn't argue with his logic. Rafe was right. There weren't many women in the Smokies, or anywhere else, like Olivia Sharp.

"Well," Janeane said doubtfully, "if you're sure."

"Let the kids go, hon. I've got to run. A new set is starting."

Janeane hung up the phone and engaged the safety on the shotgun before she set it down in the corner by the fridge. "Sorry about that. Been having some home invasions in these parts recently. Damn meth heads." She extended her hand. "Janeane Hunter."

"Olivia." Olivia shook the woman's hand. "This is my friend Jack." Jackson was Landry's middle name, and Quinn had suggested using that name instead of Cade, since it was a little less uncommon.

"You work with Seth?"

Landry could tell from the woman's smile that she liked her niece's husband. He was a little surprised, given the man's rather colorful history.

"I do," Olivia said with a smile.

"He's an interesting character," Janeane said drily. "But good people, deep down. Loves our Rachel, and he's real good to her. Have you seen pictures of the new baby?"

"Yes, ma'am," Olivia said with a laugh. "Beautiful like her mama."

Janeane beamed. "I think so, too." She caught herself up, her smile turning a little sheepish. "Here I've held you at gunpoint and now I'm talking your ear off about my little grandniece. You folks must be tired. You hungry? I could have Rafe send something from the music-hall kitchen down to the cabin."

"Actually," Olivia said, "I think we're going to head back to the music hall after we unpack. I've heard good things about the food and the entertainment."

"Well, you know I agree," Janeane said with a bright smile as she walked them to the door. "I've got to get this month's books done tonight or I'd join you." She remained on the back porch, watching while they walked to the guest cabin a few yards away.

Inside, the small cabin was clean and casually furnished with a cozy leather sofa and a pair of matching armchairs filling the front room. They explored the rest of the cabin, finding a small but complete kitchen in the back and two bedrooms, each with its own full bath, on either side of a narrow central hallway.

Unlike Olivia's cabin, which had been originally built as a tourist rental cabin and was outfitted with the sort of luxuries vacationers preferred, the Hunters' guest cabin was simpler, designed for everyday living. The bedrooms were reasonably large, but there was no hot tub on a back porch or roomy claw-foot tub in the bathrooms, just a simple toilet, tub and sink. Landry washed up, unpacked his bags and met Olivia in the front room a half hour later.

"Were you serious about going to the music hall?" he asked, noticing she'd changed out of her travel clothes into a pair of tweed trousers and a slim-fitting sweater the color of the Gulf of Mexico in the summer, a brilliant blue green reflected in her bright eyes.

"I thought it might be nice to get out and eat something besides a protein bar or a can of soup. Seth says the music's really good if you like bluegrass, and I know you do—"

"What if someone spots us?"

"You can wear that farm-supply cap I packed for you. You haven't shaved in a couple of days, and a beard always makes you look a little different. And here." She reached down and picked up a tweed newsboy cap and a pair of steel-rim glasses he hadn't noticed sitting on the coffee table nearby. She set the cap on her head, covering most of her short blond hair, and donned the glasses. "I'll wear these instead of contacts. My own mother wouldn't recognize me."

"If you don't want to be noticed, you probably shouldn't wear that sweater," he said with a wave of his hand.

She grinned so brightly at him as she took a step closer, he felt certain his heart skipped a couple of beats. "You like?"

"I love. But you'll turn every head in the place if you wear that."

She sighed. "I can keep my jacket over it. I don't want to change because it's cashmere and it's so soft."

He reached out and touched her shoulder, letting his fingers trail down her arm. She was right. The cashmere was as soft as a kitten's fur and warm from her body heat. The urge to let his fingers continue exploring the warm, soft curves of her cashmere-clad body was nearly impossible to resist.

He shoved his hands in the pockets of his jeans. "Yeah."

Those azure eyes locked with his for a long, electric moment before she looked away. "I know it's a little bit of a risk, but I'm getting cabin fever already and we just got here." Her lips curved up in the corners. "And I bet it's been a long time since you just went out and had some fun, isn't it?"

"You have no idea."

Her smile faded. "I guess I don't. I'm sorry. I didn't even think—"

He caught her cheeks between his palms, making her look at him. "It's okay. I'm glad you don't dwell on it. It helps me feel more normal, and it's been a really long time since I've felt that way."

"I know what you mean." She covered his hands with hers, holding them in place against her cheeks. "Let's just do this. Let's go, eat some good food, listen to some good music and pretend like we're both normal for a little while. What do you say?"

Impulsively, he gave her a quick, fierce hug and let her go. "Just point me to that cap and we'll get out of here."

SETH HAD TOLD Olivia the truth. The food at the Song Valley Music Hall wasn't fancy or complex, but it was delicious, fresh and prepared with care by someone who clearly knew his way around a country kitchen. The music didn't disappoint, either; the band Rafe Hunter had booked for the evening was young but wildly talented, doling out an inventive blend of bluegrass, country, rockabilly and blues that kept the patrons clapping.

After a trip to the bathroom a little after nine, Olivia returned to find the waitstaff clearing out a space in the center of the restaurant. Circling around the buzz of activity, she found Landry at their table, chatting with Rafe. Both men stood at her approach, the courtly gesture making her smile.

"What's going on?" she asked, nodding at the

hustling waiters hauling tables away from the center of the room.

"Dancing, darlin'," Rafe drawled, winking at Landry as he wandered away to talk to a couple of patrons nearby.

"Dancing, darlin'," Landry repeated, holding out his hand. "Shall we?"

She let him draw her onto the dance floor as the band fired up a brisk two-step.

"If I'd known about this place when we were both in Richmond, I would have suggested a weekend trip to check it out," he murmured in her ear a few minutes later as they swayed to a bluesy arrangement of "The Tennessee Waltz."

"Do you ever wish—" She stopped herself.

"Do I ever wish what?" he prodded when she didn't continue.

"It's stupid. Never mind."

He leaned back to look at her, his green eyes warm and soft in the mellow light of the dance hall. "No, tell me."

She took a deep breath. "Do you ever wish you could go back to the day of the warehouse explosion and do things differently?"

"Of course. All the time."

"What would you have done differently?"

"I would have questioned the order to go in, for one thing. I should have questioned it then, but I thought maybe someone had seen something inside the warehouse, some move by the bombers to take out hostages—"

"I know. I mean, I don't know what that moment was like, because I can't remember it. But I can imagine it. I think my reaction would have been the same as yours. Maybe it was. I wish I remembered."

"I'm glad you don't." His plaintive murmur made her heart hurt. "I'm glad you don't remember any of that moment. I wish I didn't."

"It wasn't your fault." She touched his cheek, enjoying the sensual scrape of his beard stubble against her palm. "You did what you were told."

"How many people's lives have been ended at the hands of someone who was just doing what he was told?" His eyes darkened to a murky forest green, his expression etched with regret. "I should've made a better choice without being told."

She dropped her hands to his shoulders and squeezed, trying to contain a sudden rush of anger for the hell he'd clearly gone through since that horrible day in Richmond. The lives lost, the careers damaged, the nightmares, the second-guessing and the ravening sense of guilt—none of it ever should have happened.

But it had. Neither of them could change a damn thing about that fact.

She kept her voice low, well aware of the crowd around them, but what she was going to say needed to be said. For her sake as well as Landry's. "Look, I know what it's like to have regrets. I get trying to figure out what you could have done differently—God knows I've pored through the notes on that case for two years now, trying to figure out what could have been done to stop any of it from happening. That's natural. But *you* didn't strap a bomb to your body and take innocent people hostage. *I* didn't hit the detonator in a room full of civilians and FBI agents. That's on those BRI bastards, not us."

"Can we get out of here?" he asked, his gaze sliding away from her face to take in the crowded music hall.

"Of course."

They called for the check, paid and tipped the server and headed out into the cold night after saying a quick good-night to Rafe on their way out.

After the doors of the music hall closed on the noise behind them, only the hiss of their frosty breaths in the night air and the thump of their shoes on the flagstones broke the frigid silence until they reached the guest cabin. Olivia unlocked the door, let them in and locked up behind them.

"Thanks," Landry said as he shrugged off his coat.

"I'm sorry. I shouldn't have pushed you to go out."

He turned quickly toward her. "No. I enjoyed it. I did. It's been a long time since I've been able to sit in a crowded restaurant with a beautiful woman, eating good food and listening to good music."

"I shouldn't have brought up Richmond."

He touched her cheek, his fingers cold against her skin. "It won't go away if we don't talk about it. It might be worse if we don't."

Taking his hand, she led him over to the sofa. She pulled him down beside her, turning to face him. "You want to talk about Richmond?"

"No. But I think I need to."

It HAD BEEN a pretty day, he remembered. Bright blue sky and mild temperatures as fall edged toward winter. The scene was so clear in his head—the sprawling warehouse south of Richmond, gleaming a creamy bone white in the midday sun, the black-clad SWAT team surrounding all the exits while the negotiation team held a tense standoff with the bombers.

"I go over and over that day in my mind. We'd been there less than two hours." He met Olivia's gentle, direct gaze. "That's nowhere near the longest we've waited for a hostage negotiation to produce results. I don't remember being tired or impatient. I just remember worrying that nothing we were doing that day was going to stop someone from dying."

Her expression was so serious, so intense, her brow furrowed as if she was trying to wring a memory from somewhere deep inside her forgetful brain. "Was there any indication that the bombers were about to make a move? I've read the incident-report files, but maybe you've remembered something since then you didn't remember at the time?"

"There was nothing. It was quiet. Eerily so. When we first got there, I could hear hostages talking and crying. But after a while, even that stopped. It was like they were resting. Holding their breaths for something to happen." He managed a faint smile. "You know that feeling."

She nodded. "The incident report said we got the order to move by radio, but the other teams said they heard no such order."

"I know. I'm not sure how it happened. Believe me, I've relived those moments a thousand times, trying to figure out how it could have happened."

"Do you remember changing the frequency at any point?"

He shook his head. "Definitely not."

"Were you in possession of your radio the whole time?"

Frowning, he replayed the moments before the radio order. He and Olivia had been on the east side of the warehouse, along with the other two agents on their team, Len Davis and Kevin Darnell. Both Davis and Darnell had died in the bomb blast. Olivia had suffered a concussion when debris had knocked her backward into a wall.

Landry's injuries had been minor scratches from shrapnel. Even though he'd been in the lead, by some fluke of fortune, he and Olivia had just moved behind a large air-conditioning unit, which took the brunt of the blast, sparing them more serious injury.

Davis and Darnell, who'd gone in the opposite direction as they started to spread out, had been hit with a blast of metal shrapnel that had killed them instantly.

Landry would never be free of those images, watching the split-second, senseless deaths of two good men. But he was damn glad Olivia had been spared that particular memory.

"Any chance someone else could have changed the radio frequency?" Olivia prodded.

He dragged his mind back to the present, meeting her curious gaze. "Yes. There was. I don't know why I didn't consider that possibility."

She licked her lips. "When?"

"Just about fifteen minutes before all hell broke loose, Agent Boyle came by with water. Remember?" He kicked himself when she ruefully shook her head. "I'm sorry. Of course you don't. It was the first time we'd seen him all morning. I guess I must have assumed he was back at the staging area, conferring with the negotiators. He gave us each pep talks."

She frowned. "Boyle gave us pep talks?"

"I know that wasn't his way, but we both know the way he felt about domestic terrorists. He was rabid, and that's kind of what the pep talks were about. He told me, and I guess he told the rest of you, too, that whatever happened, we were patriots for trying to stop the bombers."

She shook her head. "Patriots. Interesting choice of words, now that we know he was working with the BRI to stage a big incident."

"In retrospect, I have to wonder if he didn't stage the incident in Richmond."

"Or maybe it was just a target of opportunity. Maybe he let his zealotry get the better of him and took advantage of the situation to create an incident."

"We weren't supposed to live, were we?"

She met his gaze solemnly. "I don't think we were. When we did, and you told the debriefers about the radio call, it sounded like a lie."

"A bad agent covering his ass." Landry shook his head. "And suddenly the story became about FBI malpractice instead of a domestic terror attack. No wonder Boyle sabotaged me. He must have been so furious."

"You said it was the main negotiator, Williams, you heard on the radio. Are you sure it wasn't Boyle?"

"As sure as you can be about a voice over a radio. I didn't know Williams that well, but he has that distinctive Brooklyn accent. Definitely not a Baltimore accent like Boyle had."

"Their voices are around the same depth, though," Olivia murmured. "A Brooklyn accent is so distinctive, it's easy to mimic, especially over a radio. And none of us on the team were from Brooklyn, so it's not like we'd have been able to distinguish a real accent from a fake one."

He followed her unspoken logic. "Fifteen minutes before the radio call, Boyle came by and took us one by one to talk to us. I remember he put his hands on my shoulders because at one point, he made my shoulder radio squawk with static, and I nearly jumped out of my skin."

"He was changing the radio frequency." Olivia let out a soft curse. "The bastard set us all up to be killed for his obsession."

A shivery sense of relief washed over Landry, spreading goose bumps along his arms and legs. In the rush of excitement, he reached up and cradled Olivia's face between his palms. "That's it. Oh, baby, that's exactly how it happened. You have no idea how much that question has haunted me. How did I not see it before?"

She closed her hands over his. "You just needed your partner to help you talk it out."

Emotion swelled in his chest, choking him. A flurry of thoughts, of images and pent-up feelings, swirled through his brain, but the lump in his throat wouldn't let them come out in words.

But he could see those unspoken thoughts shining in Olivia's eyes.

Two words finally escaped his tight throat. "I forgot."

Her lips trembled in a whisper of a smile. "Forgot what?"

"Us. I forgot us." Swept up in an irresistible whirlwind of emotion, he curled his hand around the back of her neck and pulled her closer, fitting his mouth to hers.

The first time he'd kissed her after so long apart, it had seemed like kissing a beautiful stranger. The desire had been there, but not the familiarity. Not the sense of knowing.

The second kiss, initiated by Olivia, had been an explosion of fiery desire, almost faceless and nameless in its intensity. Two mouths, two bodies, looking for pleasure and completion.

But this kiss, this melding of lips and tangling of tongues, this symphony of touches and breaths and long, deep sighs—

This kiss felt like home.

Chapter Fourteen

Us, she thought. *This is us.*

Landry's hands moved in a slow, sweet exploration of her face before sliding down to her shoulders and sweeping lightly down her arms. His fingers clasped hers. Entwined with them. And it felt so familiar, so perfect, that she wondered how they ever could have let go of this sense of completeness.

She let go of his hands and lifted her fingers to his face, tracing the little nicks and contours she'd once known as intimately as she knew her own face. That scar on his chin was a high school baseball injury, when he'd taken a cleat to the face diving to tag out a runner stealing base. The dimples that creased his cheeks when he laughed had come from his grandfather on his mother's side, he'd once told her, though his mother didn't have dimples.

"At least, I don't think she did," he'd said when she'd asked about the dimples that still had the power to make her heart skip a beat. "I never saw that much of her, and when I did, she wasn't smiling."

The image of his distant, unsmiling mother made her heart break a little each time she thought of it.

She drew back from the kiss, opening her eyes. Landry stared back at her, his gaze soft but intense. Slowly, he smiled, triggering the dimples, and she couldn't stop a soft laugh.

"What?" he asked.

"Those dimples."

His smile widened, the dimples deepening. "Missed 'em, did you?"

"I did."

"I missed *you*. Every single inch of you."

"All seventy of them?"

He laughed. "Yeah. And even more when you're wearing heels."

She pressed her forehead against his. "How did we let it fall apart? One day we were fine, and the next—"

"I don't think we were fine." He leaned back, putting a little distance between them. Cool air seeped in between them, giving her a chill.

She rubbed her arms. "You're right. We weren't."

"This is such a bad time to be considering this." He rubbed his jaw, his palm rasping against his beard stubble. "I have no idea what's going to happen next. I'm wanted by the FBI, and you've been targeted by the BRI, and in case it's not clear, those bastards aren't going to just let me go unscathed if I run into one of them in the woods one day and they figure out who I am."

"All the more reason we should stick together." She lifted her chin and pinned him with her more determined gaze. "Maybe it'll all go wrong again. Hell, maybe it's inevitable. But right now we need each other, as partners if nothing else. We just work better together than apart, and you know it. Tell me I'm wrong."

"You're not wrong." He bent toward her and pressed his lips against her forehead. She snuggled closer and he wrapped his arms around her, holding her close. "I just don't think we need to get ourselves all tangled up in plans and promises when we're not sure what tomorrow's going to hold."

She sighed, wishing she could argue with his logic. But he was right. Rushing into things never worked out well, in her experience. "Okay. We'll slow it down and just concentrate on the work for now. Agents Landry and Sharp, back on the job."

"That sounds good." He gave her a quick kiss on the temple then let her go. "In the morning, that is. It's late and we've had a few long, stressful days. Let's get some sleep and we'll get started first thing in the morning. Deal?"

"Deal." She extended her hand toward him.

He shook her hand, his grip lasting a little longer than necessary. In his green eyes she saw a sweet, intense longing that echoed in her own chest. Finally, he let go and smiled. "I really did miss the hell out of you."

"Back at ya." She made herself turn around and head for the bedroom she'd staked out earlier in the evening, closing the door behind her. By the time she'd snuggled under the warm blankets, she heard Landry's footsteps enter the hall outside her room.

His footsteps faltered as he neared her door. Olivia waited, breathless, for him to make another move.

When his footsteps moved on, and the door to his bedroom opened and closed, she let out a pent-up breath, well aware he'd made the smart decision.

But she didn't have to like it.

Her cell phone hummed on the bedside table where she'd left it. It wasn't her normal phone; she'd left that back at The Gates locked in her desk. Instead, Quinn had provided both her and Landry with untraceable burner phones for their trip to Bryson City. Her late-night caller could be only one person.

"It's nearly midnight, Quinn," she said into the phone.

"You didn't check in when you arrived."

He was right. She hadn't. "Sorry."

"Everything okay?"

"Everything's fine," she assured him, tucking her knees up to her chest. "No problems on the road, got here in time to have some good food and listen to some good music and now we're safely tucked in our beds for the night."

Quinn was silent for a long moment.

"Is something wrong?" she asked when he didn't speak.

"Are you alone in that bed?"

Her spine straightened. "Is that any business of yours?"

"No. Not the way you mean."

"Then in what way *is* it your business?"

"I remember the Olivia Sharp who walked into my office looking for a job. She was— I'm not sure I even know the right word for it. Broken, I guess. Not in a way that was obvious. But there were pieces missing, and I could see it."

"Thank you for the analysis, Dr. Phil."

"I'm not trying to psychoanalyze you, Olivia. I'm not sticking my nose where it doesn't belong. If you're going to continue to be a vital member of my team, you have to be smart and focused and emotionally centered."

"I am all of those things."

"Good. Keep it that way." Quinn's voice lowered. "I take it from your answers that you really are alone in your room?"

"Quinn—"

He laughed softly. "That time, I was sticking my nose where it doesn't belong."

"I'm fine," she said, realizing he'd thrown in the last question just to break the tension. "And I know what I'm doing. I promise."

"I hope whatever happens with Landry is a good thing for you. I really do. But I need you to put your own safety first. Carver's missing, and for all we know, he's already dead. I don't want to have to call up your mother and tell her that you're gone, too."

She tamped down a flush of guilt. She hadn't talked to her mother in over a week, she realized. Carla Sharp hadn't exactly been a great role model, but Olivia had never once doubted her mother loved her. And she loved her mother, too, even when Carla exasperated her beyond words. Maybe especially then.

"I don't want you to have to do that, either," she said. "I'll be careful."

"You do that," Quinn said. "Call if you need anything."

"Will do." She hung up, set the phone on the bedside table and stared up at the darkened ceiling, wondering if she was going to be able to keep her word. Carver was missing; she and Landry were both hunted. She'd chosen the work she did willingly, knowing the dangers, but she was nearly thirty-five now. Her window of opportunity for having a child of her own was closing quickly, if having a child was even what she wanted.

Was it? She and Landry had been partners and lovers, but one thing they'd never seriously talked about was getting married and starting a family. In fact, in retrospect, she could see that they'd gone out of their way to avoid talking about marriage and kids.

Why? What had they been afraid of? That they wanted different things out of life? In some ways, she knew Landry as well as she knew anyone in the world, but in others, she didn't think she knew him at all.

Because he'd wanted it that way? Because she had?

Maybe they were crazy to think they could make their relationship work this time.

Maybe they were crazy to try.

OLIVIA WAS ALREADY up the next morning, scrambling eggs, when he wandered into the kitchen. She turned around to flash him a quick smile. "Good morning."

Her face was freshly scrubbed and free of makeup, and her hair was damp and tousled from the shower, but she was still the most beautiful thing he'd ever seen, especially in that Alabama T-shirt and houndstooth-patterned running shorts, her long, tanned legs stretching for miles beneath the hem.

"Good morning," he replied, looking over her shoulder. "Need any help?"

"The toaster is over there on the counter. There's bread in the pantry—the Hunters stocked the place with some essentials for us, it seems. Janeane left a note so we'd know everything's fresh."

The kind gesture touched him more than it probably should have. "That was nice of her."

Olivia must have heard something odd in his tone, for she turned away from the stove to look at him. "It was."

He smiled. "I guess it's been a while since I've experienced much human kindness."

Olivia reached out and touched his arm briefly. "Give yourself a little time to get used to it again." She turned back to the eggs.

He hoped he'd have reason to get used to it. The thought of returning to a life of running and hiding was deeply disheartening. He'd grown accustomed to living a mostly solitary life, his only relationships shallow and transient.

But he'd never grown to like it.

The toaster took four slices at once. He put bread in the slots and pushed down the lever. "If we can't figure out a way to prove someone in the FBI set me up, I'll have to go back under the radar."

"We'll figure it out," she said, her voice firm.

"You can't know that."

She moved the skillet from the stove eye and turned to look at him. "I will not rest until we figure it out."

God, he loved her when she stuck out her chin and made declarations of intent. She was fierce and formidable and as sexy as hell.

He lifted his own chin in response. "Then neither will I."

She flashed him a big, toothy grin. "There's the Cade Landry I remember."

He hoped she was right. He hoped he was the man he used to be, because the man he'd become didn't seem to be a damned bit of good to anyone.

As they were cleaning up after breakfast, Olivia outlined her plan for the morning. "I brought files with me that I want you to go through. They're dossiers we've gathered on the bigger players in the Blue Ridge Infantry, and I was hoping maybe you could tell us if any of them were involved in your abduction."

"I didn't see faces. They wore masks."

"Maybe there will be something else that you'll be able to identify about them. Or maybe something in their files will spark a memory." She put the last cup in the dishwasher and straightened. "I set up everything for us in the front room."

He followed her into the living area and saw that she'd stacked fifteen manila folders in a neat line on the long coffee table in front of the sofa. "How long have you been awake?"

"A couple of hours." She slanted a sheepish smile at him as she took a seat on one end of the sofa. "Early riser, remember?"

"I remember." He sat beside her and picked up the first dossier. "Calvin Hopkins."

"Head of the Tennessee branch of the Blue Ridge Infantry. Anything familiar about him?" Olivia asked as he flipped open the folder.

The photos in the dossier appeared to be candid shots taken with a telephoto lens. "Who took these shots?"

"Grant Carver, among others," she answered soberly. "One of the benefits of his living near the Fowler Ridge enclave."

"If you know where they're living, why hasn't someone gone in and staged a raid?"

"Because they learned a little something from the meth cookers with whom they've aligned themselves. They don't bring their drug business home. We think they've set up meth labs in other places in the hills. Abandoned cabins up high in the hills, maybe. Or even some of the old, abandoned marble quarries north of here. A few of those places are still private property, with absentee owners. All kinds of activity could be going on there without anybody but a few locals knowing it."

Landry rubbed his jaw, realizing he was already falling back into the habit of not shaving. Reentering civilization after nearly a year of living on the fringes was proving to be more difficult than he'd expected.

"Take a close look at some of the people with Hopkins," Olivia suggested as he flipped to a photo of Hopkins talking to a clean-shaven man wearing khakis and a light blue golf shirt. "That guy isn't in the BRI, we're pretty sure."

"Maybe he's just some tourist asking for directions."

"Maybe. Or maybe he's one of those other FBI agents Darryl Boyle spoke about before he disappeared."

He looked up at her, frowning. "What other FBI agents?"

"You said you thought there was someone in the FBI who had contacted the BRI when you tried to report Boyle's treachery to your superiors. I just figured you knew that Boyle wasn't the only one."

"I did but I didn't realize Boyle had actually admitted it." Landry looked at the photo of the man in the khakis. "I don't recognize him. Do you?"

She shook her head. "But I left the FBI before you did. I was hoping maybe he was someone in one of the local field offices. Probably not an agent, but maybe one of the support staff?"

"He might be with the Knoxville office, I

guess," Landry said doubtfully. "Though you'd think Rigsby would have recognized him."

"She didn't."

"If he was with the Johnson City RA, he was either there before I came aboard or after I left."

Olivia sighed. "I guess it was too much to hope for."

"Sorry."

She shook her head. "Don't be. We have a lot more files to go."

They continued working their way through the files, concentrating on photographs first. Then when none of those pictures triggered any memories, they started to go through the written reports The Gates had gathered from their agents as well as civilians who lived or worked in areas influenced by the Blue Ridge Infantry.

"Your files are amazingly thorough," Landry commented a couple of hours later when they stopped for a break. She had coaxed him into his jacket and boots for a walk in the woods behind the guesthouse, where the evergreens had sheltered much of the remaining snow from the melting rays of the sun.

"Unfortunately, we've had a lot of run-ins with members of the Blue Ridge Infantry. And a few of their drug-dealer and anarchist buddies."

"I'm not sure the FBI's files on these groups are as detailed."

"The BRI has become really savvy about cov-

ering their tracks. We can outline how we think
they're committing crimes, but producing evidence of their involvement is another thing altogether."

"I know. I was part of a task force trying to
round some of them up, remember?"

"Right." She gave him a sidelong look. "You
never told me how you were working with the
BRI. I know you weren't sanctioned to get involved with the BRI undercover while you were
on that task force. When Quinn got us involved
in trying to keep McKenna Rigsby safe, we did
a lot of digging with our FBI sources and we
found out that much. But you ended up working
with them anyway. How did it happen?"

"The contact fell into my lap. A guy who lived
in the apartment next door was doing some jobs
for them. Transporting contraband, that kind of
thing. They made a mistake with him—he wasn't
a meth head, but he was a drinker, and when he
got drunk, he liked to talk. I figured out that I
could pick his brains easily enough if I made
sure to be his designated driver. So I ended up
spending my nights at his favorite bars, looking
for a chance to scrape him up off his bar stool
and take him home."

"What kind of information did he give you?"

"Upcoming runs for the BRI. When they'd be
moving drugs from one place to another. I went
to Chang and told him what was up. I figured

we could interdict the next run, if that's the way they wanted to go, but they didn't think there was sufficient evidence to warrant a raid." He frowned at the memory.

"That's ridiculous," she said, sounding confused. "What was their reasoning?"

"They didn't say. And I wasn't in any position to push them on it, given my shaky status with the Bureau." He shook his head, angry with himself. "I should have pushed anyway. I knew there was something hinky going on. But I just—I just didn't much care at the time."

"You must have started caring at some point, if you ended up working with the BRI anyway."

He nodded. "I did."

"What happened?"

"Rigsby disappeared."

The curious look she sent his way was tinged with suspicion. "I knew you were part of the team running her undercover op, but I wasn't aware you'd become close."

He almost laughed at the thought. "We weren't close. But I knew she was a good agent. She certainly didn't go rogue for the hell of it, so I knew something had gone really wrong. And I might not have been running on all cylinders as an agent, but my gut told me that whatever had gone wrong had gone wrong on the FBI end of the operation."

"What did you do?"

"I tried to get Chang to let me go undercover

and see what had gone wrong. I had a ready way in, through my neighbor, and I was still pretty new to Tennessee, so it wasn't like anyone in the BRI would know my face. At least, that's what I figured. I didn't know about Boyle at that time."

"Chang said no?"

"He ran it up the Bureau chain of command and came back with a no," Landry corrected her. "I think he might have contacted the Knoxville field office and got the no-go from Boyle. He was the Knoxville liaison person."

"So he would have known you were trying to go undercover. He must have tipped off the BRI."

"That's the thing. I don't think he told them anything. At least, not at first." Snow crunched beneath their boots as they hiked through the woods, stretching their limbs. Landry's legs were still a little sore from their long hike over the mountain, but the exercise helped loosen the aching muscles and tendons.

"It must have suited his purposes for you to go undercover," Olivia mused. "Do you know why?"

Landry shook his head. "When Rigsby called me to meet her at the Econo-Tel, I had a gut feeling I shouldn't follow protocol. But I just didn't trust my instincts. Instead, I went through proper FBI channels. I called our task-force liaison to report the contact."

"Darryl Boyle."

"I knew when he told me not to contact anyone

else, something was wrong. I even tried reaching Chang, but I never got through."

"So you called the number Rigsby had used to contact you, trying to warn her about Boyle."

He nodded. "I got Nick Darcy instead. By then, Boyle was already on his way to the other meet site Rigsby set up, along with some of his BRI buddies."

"So you knew then that whatever contacts you'd made in the BRI were compromised."

"I knew I couldn't trust Boyle. So I went home to pack some things. I knew I couldn't stay there anymore. I went to the bank and got a few thousand dollars out. Stashed it somewhere safe where I could access it if I needed to. I contacted my landlord and broke my lease. Told him to keep the deposit for his trouble."

"That made you look like you were on the run."

"I was." He looked at her. "I had no idea who to trust. Or if there was anybody left at all who could help me."

"You could have contacted *me*." The look she gave him was half fury, half dismay, as if she wasn't sure whether she wanted to give him a whack upside the head or burst into tears.

"I wanted to. I knew you were working for The Gates, so I knew where to find you. But I made a mistake."

"What mistake?"

"I gave the FBI another chance."

Chapter Fifteen

"Who did you contact?" Olivia asked, dread settling in the pit of her belly. Since leaving the FBI, she'd taken her share of emotional blows where the people she'd worked with were concerned. First Boyle. Then for a while, she'd come to fear that Landry was a traitor, too.

"I went over Chang's head," Landry answered. "Called someone at FBI headquarters instead. Dallas Cole."

Her eyebrows lifted a notch at the name. Dallas Cole? "The visual-information specialist at headquarters?"

Landry smiled at her surprise. "Yeah. Exactly. I figured, who would bother to corrupt a guy who designs brochures?"

She tried to picture upright Dallas Cole taking a bribe. "You're not telling me someone did."

"Honestly, I don't know. I haven't tried to contact him again to see what happened, for obvious reasons. He was always a pretty straight arrow—maybe he didn't listen when I told him to skip the chain of command and go straight to Assistant Director Crandall to tell him where to contact me."

"Actually, the Dallas Cole I remember wouldn't break chain-of-command protocol for anyone," Olivia said. "And if Boyle had thought ahead and made a few calls…"

Landry sighed. "Cole would have reported my contact and they'd know where to find me. Which must be exactly what he did. Because it wasn't twenty minutes later, while I was waiting for a call back from Crandall, that a bunch of big, bearded guys ambushed me and hauled me off for interrogation."

Olivia touched his arm, horrified by the pictures his words painted in her mind. "No wonder you didn't think there was anyone in the FBI you could trust."

"Now you know why I didn't turn myself in to the authorities when I got away from my captors."

"I'm sorry. I'm so sorry you felt so alone. That you didn't feel there was anyone you could trust."

He touched her hand then gently removed it from his arm and took a few steps away. "We should probably get back."

"Wait." She tugged him around to face her, not ready to let him leave. Not before she told him what she'd spent most of the night before thinking about. "You know what we said last night, about the wisdom of trying to recapture what we had together?"

He met her gaze with wary eyes. "Yeah?"

She took a deep breath. "I don't think we should try."

His eyes flickered, as if she'd caught him flat-footed. "Oh."

She realized he didn't get what she was saying. "I'm sorry. I didn't say that well. What I mean is, we aren't the same people. I know I'm not, and I think you'd agree that you're not, either. Right?"

His expression shuttered. "Right."

He started to turn away from her, but she was still holding his hand.

"So let's not try to recapture our relationship." She caught his other hand in hers and stepped closer until her heat enveloped him. "Let's make something new."

She let go of his hands and rose to kiss him, her arms wrapping around his shoulders to pull him closer. As Landry tightened his arms around her waist and pulled her flush to his body, the cold dissipated. The rustle of wind in the trees disappeared, swallowed by the thunderous pounding of Olivia's pulse in her ears.

It was so easy to let herself be swept up in the memories of their time together, the whirlwind of crazy hours, high-octane SWAT missions and stolen moments of pleasure in a world sometimes gone insane. They'd lived on passion and adrenaline, glossing over the missing pieces of their relationship as if they didn't matter. Things like trust and commitment, the building blocks of a relationship that had lasting power.

No wonder it had all fallen apart.

As if he sensed her sudden doubts, Landry's grip on her loosened, and he drew back to meet her gaze, his green eyes troubled. "What's wrong?"

"We made so many mistakes before."

His lips pressed flat as he nodded. "I know."

"I don't want to make those mistakes again."

He let her go, turning so that his profile was to her. "Okay. I get that. We should probably go back to the cabin and get back to work anyway."

"That's not what I mean." She moved closer to him, missing the heat of his body. "I want it to work this time. Don't you?"

He turned slowly to look at her. "Of course."

"We never thought past the next day." She shook her head. "Hell, most of the time we never thought past the next hour. We lived in the here and now, and we thought it was enough. But it wasn't. Was it?"

"No." He shook his head. "It wasn't nearly enough."

"If we do this, I don't want to settle for less than everything."

"You mean marriage and kids and mortgages?" His expression shuttered, and she felt the first hard flush of dismay.

But before she could answer him, she felt a quiet buzz against her hip. "Damn it." She pulled her vibrating phone from her pocket. It was Alexander Quinn, of course.

"What, does he have you wired for sound?" Landry muttered as she pushed the answer button.

"Hello?"

"Carver showed up at home, a little scuffed but okay."

Relief swamped her. "That's amazing news! Did he escape?"

"Carver?" Landry asked softly. She nodded.

"Yes, but I'm not a hundred percent sure they didn't let him go."

"Why do you say that?"

"Because he came back with a message. And I think maybe it was one they wanted him to deliver."

"What kind of message?"

Quinn's voice lowered. "You're not on speaker, are you?"

Olivia glanced at Landry. "No."

"Carver said the men who took him told him there's a reason Cade Landry came out of hiding and sought you out. That the story he told you about being a target is true. But it's not the Blue Ridge Infantry who's after you."

"Then who?"

"It's Landry."

SOMETHING WAS WRONG. Very, very wrong. From the sudden shift in Olivia's posture to the blank expression on her face, Landry knew that whatever Quinn was telling her had hit her like a brick bat.

Was it something about Carver? Had something bad happened back in Purgatory?

"That's not possible." She spoke in a careful tone, still looking at Landry even as her expression remained frozen in neutral.

Whatever Quinn said to her didn't do anything to improve her demeanor. She finally looked away, her gaze going south toward the guest cabin barely visible through the trees.

"I understand. You don't have to worry." She hung up the phone and took a deep breath before she slowly turned to look at him.

"Carver's okay?"

"He escaped. He was a little beat up, but Quinn says he's going to be fine." Something in her voice suggested she wasn't telling him the whole story, but she turned and started walking toward the cabin before he could ask anything else.

He hurried to catch up. "Wait a minute— what else was Quinn telling you? What's he worried about?"

"I'll tell you when we get to the cabin," she answered, picking up her pace until they were almost jogging through the trees.

The hair on the back of his neck rose as she beat him inside and disappeared almost immediately into her bedroom and closed the door. Adrenaline pumped into his system, feeding his rising alarm.

Get the Kimber, his instincts screamed. *Get it now.*

He pushed down the rising fear, held it in check. This was Olivia. Whatever had gone down between them, she wouldn't hurt him. Not without reason. He had to believe that, or he had nothing at all to believe in anymore.

Remaining where he stood in the middle of the front room of the guest cabin, he waited, his ragged breathing slowly subsiding and his pounding heart easing to a slow, steady beat.

When the door of her bedroom opened, the click of the latch sent a little jolt through his nervous system, but he fought against the fight-or-flight instinct and made himself remain still while she slowly emerged from the hallway and walked back into the front room.

She was holding her Glock in her right hand, the barrel facing the floor. Moisture glistened in her eyes but she wasn't crying. He could see the effort it was taking not to let the tears fall.

She didn't look at him as she spoke. "Quinn

thinks the BRI let Carver escape on purpose. He said that Carver overheard something his captors said, and Quinn thinks they planned it that way. They wanted to give us a message without delivering it directly."

Landry swallowed with difficulty. "What message?" he asked, though he had a sick feeling he already knew.

"He heard them say they're not the ones who are after me."

The cold certainty deepened, rippled like an icy breeze down his limbs, scattering goose bumps. "Then who is?"

Olivia's gaze lifted and locked with his. "You. They said it's you."

He saw pain in her eyes, and his heart contracted. Did she believe Quinn? Was that why she was carrying the Glock?

For her protection against him?

She lifted the Glock and he braced for whatever came next, knowing he couldn't do anything that might hurt her, no matter what she did next. When she set the Glock on the top of the glass-front cabinet that stood against the wall and dropped her empty hands to her sides, he released his pent-up breath.

"Landry, the one thing I know, the one thing I believe with absolute certainty, is that you didn't come in from the cold in order to hurt me."

Relief rolled through him, threatening to make his knees buckle.

She took a step closer, her gaze holding steady with his. "I'm not sure what the BRI is up to by sending a message through Carver the way they did. Maybe it's an attempt to turn us all against each other. Or maybe whatever operation you overheard them planning that day through the bedroom vent wasn't a sanctioned BRI operation, and this is their way of letting us know. I honestly don't know. But I know you. No matter what went wrong, no matter how many problems we overlooked instead of fixed, no matter how much time we've spent apart, I know you. You won't hurt me, because it would kill you. Just like I won't hurt you."

He glanced at the Glock she'd laid on the cabinet and forced a smile. "I have to admit, I wasn't so sure you weren't going to hurt me the other day when you pulled your shotgun on me."

She smiled back, the tears welling in her eyes trickling down her cheeks. "I had the safety on. You didn't notice?"

"I couldn't see past the barrel stuck in my face." He took another deep breath and let it out. "So the BRI is spreading the word that I'm the big bad, huh? I guess Quinn was pretty quick to buy into it?"

"Quinn's not exactly the trusting sort."

"You don't say." He walked back to the front

door of the cabin and looked outside, scanning the yard. The sun was already high in the sky, hot enough despite the chilly temperatures to melt away half the snow that had been in the yard that morning when he woke. "Does the BRI have any idea where we are?"

"I don't know. Sometimes I think they have every inch of the Appalachians under surveillance."

"How much do you trust Quinn?"

"Enough," she said after a moment's thought. "You asked if he believes this story about you. I think by calling me, he gave us the answer."

"He believes it."

"Actually, no. I don't think he does. He gave me the choice of what to do by calling me. If he truly believed you were the bad guy in this scenario, he and a dozen other agents from The Gates would have shown up without warning and gotten me out of here before calling the FBI to come get you."

"So that call was about giving you the facts at hand and trusting you to make the right decision?"

"That's how Quinn works. He says he has to be able to trust his agents to make the right decision in the field."

"So what's your decision in the field?"

"I think we're about as safe here, for the moment, as we'd be anywhere." She looked around the cabin, her eyes narrowed as if she were assessing the cabin's utility as a fortress. "I wouldn't mind shoring up our defenses a bit, though."

"What do you have in mind?"

"Short of building a moat?" She flashed him a grin that made his heart flip-flop, and for a second, he felt as if he'd been transported to three years earlier, when they had still been together, still partners. Still lovers.

He forced himself back to the present. She had been right earlier, when she'd said it was folly to try to recapture the past. The past, for all its delights, had also been riddled with mistakes and lost opportunities.

They had a chance to start fresh. And that was what he planned to do.

"How much do you think we can trust Rafe and Janeane?" he asked.

"Seth Hammond trusts them. And he's a pretty good judge of character. He made his living off being able to read people, you know."

"Interesting choice of hires for The Gates," he murmured.

"Quinn's a pretty good judge of character, too." She crossed to him and took his hand. "We're going to figure all of this out. You're not going to spend the rest of your life running. Do you hear me?"

When she said it, he could almost believe it. "I hear you."

"We've just got to figure out a plan. Something more proactive than hunkering down and hoping nobody finds us. Making this place or any other place a fortress is the same as making it a prison. I have no desire to live the rest of my life in a prison."

She never had been the wait-and-see type, he thought. It didn't seem that the time they'd spent apart had quelled her propensity to take action.

Waiting had never been one of his strong suits, either. Which was why he'd spent the previous night working out potential plans of action in his head when sleep proved elusive.

Putting his life in the hands of the FBI wasn't something he was willing to try again, even if it was unfair to the thousands of honest, trustworthy agents and staffers in the Bureau's employ. He didn't know who could be trusted, so he had to work on the premise that he could trust none of them.

But Olivia was right. He may have escaped BRI captivity months ago, but that didn't mean he wasn't still trapped behind the invisible bars of life on the run.

It was time to come out of hiding.

"You have something in mind, don't you?" Her eyes narrowed a twitch, a faint smile playing with her lips. "Come on, Landry. Spill."

"I do have something in mind," he admitted as he crossed to the fireplace and added logs and kindling to the cold hearth. Despite the rising temperatures that continued to melt the blanket of snow outside, the cabin was chilly, sending shivers down his spine.

Or maybe it was the plan he'd been formulating that was giving him the shakes. Because he'd figured out last night, lying in a strange bed in the dark, listening to the moans of the wind in the eaves and the thud of his own pulse in his ears, that there would be no easy solution to his problem.

He was a wanted man, and he had no proof of his contentions about what had happened almost a year ago when he'd tried to do the right thing and had ended up bound and beaten for his efforts.

The only way out was to get the proof.

And the only way to get proof was to bait a trap.

"Are you going to tell me or not?" Olivia's voice was close behind him, her breath warm against his neck.

"I can't prove I'm not a traitor. Because I can't prove I was set up. Especially not while I'm hunkered down and hiding."

Suddenly, she was standing in front of him, her eyes wide and scared. "What exactly are you suggesting?"

He took her hands in his. "It was my fault that McKenna Rigsby's plan to trap Darryl Boyle went sideways."

"Because you followed protocol and contacted Boyle in his capacity as the task-force liaison?" Olivia's grip on his hands tightened. "How were you supposed to know he was one of the bad guys?"

"I think I did know, deep down," he said bleakly. "But that's not what I'm trying to get at." He tugged her hands up, pressing her knuckles against his chest. "I'm saying that if I hadn't screwed up and called Boyle, her plan might have worked. Boyle wouldn't have been forewarned, and he might have walked right into Rigsby's trap. It was a good plan. It just might be a great plan."

"You want to set a trap."

"Yes."

Her voice rasped. "With you as bait."

Chapter Sixteen

"This is a crazy idea."

Stopping in the middle of making notes on the files he was studying, Landry slanted a look Olivia's way. "Just an hour ago, you agreed it would work."

She put her hands over his, tugging the pen from his fingers. "I said it *could* work. Could is not would."

He closed his eyes. "Livvie."

"Don't Livvie me, Cade Landry. You're already working out the logistics of a plan when we haven't even considered other options."

"What other options?" He pushed aside the notepad and turned to face her, his expression tight with exasperation. "There are no other options. I've known since I got away that one day, sooner or later, I was going to have to put myself out there as a lure to get the BRI and their friends in the FBI to show their hands. It's time to stop avoiding the inevitable."

"I think you're being reckless."

"And I think you don't want to face the fact that there's no safe way out of this mess. Not for me, anyway." He took the pen from her grip. "I still think it might be a good idea for you to call Quinn to come get you. Take you back to The Gates until whatever happens to me happens."

Anger burned lava-hot in the center of her chest. "Who do you think I am? Do I look like the kind of person who would hide behind the walls of The Gates to save myself while you're out there with your neck on the line? Do you think I could do that to the man I—" She bit off the word, not quite ready to say it aloud, even though the emotion swelled in her chest, threatening to burst forth no matter how hard she tried to keep it bottled up.

He cradled her cheeks between his palms, gentle understanding in his gaze. "No. I know you couldn't. But I'm not the man who could let you risk your life without trying to talk you out of it."

She pressed her forehead to his. "We should call Quinn, at least. Get some backup for this operation."

"Livvie, you've told me yourself that you've had leaks at the agency."

"But we stopped the leaker."

"You stopped *a* leaker. Are you sure there aren't other traitors in your midst?"

As much as she wished she could say she was

sure, she wasn't. Not really. There hadn't been any sign of information leaks since the police had taken Marty Tucker into custody after he'd tried to kill Anson and Ginny Daughtry when they'd figured out his secret. But that didn't mean there wasn't another mole in the agency biding his time before he could make a move.

"No," she admitted. "I don't think there is. I really don't. But I can't be a hundred percent sure."

"Then we do it my way."

"How exactly are we going to document what happens when the bad guys spring the trap? We're not exactly rolling in cash or audiovisual equipment." She gave him a pointed look.

"There's a music hall not a hundred yards from here that has its own recording equipment."

Her brow furrowed with suspicion. "And you know this how?"

"When you went to the ladies' room last night, I chatted a bit with Rafe. You remember that balcony that goes around the whole music hall, kind of like those old-timey Western saloons?"

"Yeah?"

"I noticed there was a guy up there recording the music sets. I was curious, so I asked Rafe about it. He said he invested in some audio and video equipment a couple of years ago when he started working with talent agents to get their clients' work in front of prospective record labels.

They pay him to record the sets live, and those sets go on public video-sharing sites. They can only upload the ones where the artists still retain the rights to the music, but Rafe said it's gotten several of the bands who debut here a closer look from the record labels looking for fresh talent."

"And you think Rafe will just hand over his expensive equipment to you for your sting?"

"I hope so."

"And if he doesn't?"

"I still have some money left over from the funds I took out of our joint bank account the other day. I'd just rather not tap into it if I don't have to." He flashed a smile. "Might need it for bail money."

"If this plan doesn't work," she muttered, "you're not likely to be granted bail."

He put down the pen, pushed his notes away and pulled her into his lap. She snuggled closer as he wrapped his arms around her waist and buried his face in her neck. "We have to try something, Livvie. This waiting for something to happen is going to kill me."

She kissed the top of his head, wishing she could argue. But he was right. He'd already spent nearly a year in hiding, and the longer it went on, the more dangerous it would become. He needed his life back.

She needed *him* back.

"I think you may be right about backup,

though." He leaned his head back to look at her. "We have no idea how many people might be involved in the FBI branch of the Blue Ridge Infantry. If it's more than two, we'll be outnumbered."

"I don't want to be outnumbered. We don't have to be."

"I know you trust the people you work with."

"I want to trust the people I work with," she corrected him bleakly. "But after this past year and the leaks—"

"You said you thought you'd caught the only leaker."

"And you asked me if I was sure, and I said no."

"I've been thinking about that, too." He rubbed his chin against her collarbone, his beard prickling her skin, sending lovely little shivers of sexual awareness skittering down her spine. "Everybody who was in that conference room yesterday knows where we are. You trusted them enough not to change our plans."

She thought about the men and women who'd helped them figure out the logistics of their trip to Bryson City. She would trust her life to any of them. Perhaps more to the point, she'd trust Landry's life to any of them. "I did. I do."

"So they're the ones we contact. But I don't want to go through the phone system at The Gates or their cell phones. If there is a leaker at your agency, they might have access to anything that could be connected directly to the company. Do you have other ways to contact them?"

She had home phone numbers for most of them in the address-book app in her phone, coded in case someone ever managed to sneak a peek at the saved information. "I do."

"Good. We can call them when we get our plans finalized. Tell them how they can help." He gave her hip a little slap. "As tempting as it is to cuddle here with you on the sofa, we have to work out a lot of logistics."

She sighed and slid out of his grasp, settling on the sofa next to him. "Starting with figuring out if Dallas Cole is still with the FBI."

ICE CRUSTED ON the banks of the Potomac, an incongruous contrast with the cloud-streaked brilliance of the January sunset, reflected in all its fiery glory in the glassy surface of the river. The Jefferson Memorial was little more than a murky silhouette in the distance, a reminder that for all the beauty of its natural surroundings, Washington, DC, was a city built on power. Powerful men, powerful institutions, powerful ambition and powerful greed.

He had seen it all during his time in the capital. Idealism had died a million deaths on the altar of compromise. Good intentions soon became swallowed by desperation to score an elusive win at any cost.

Governing a free country could be a very nasty business, indeed.

He sighed and spoke into the phone. "When did you get the call?"

"Ten minutes ago." The voice on the other line was deep and well modulated, though even if he hadn't known the speaker already, he'd have been able to detect the hint of eastern Kentucky in the man's inflections.

Dallas Cole had tried to leave coal country behind him, but there were things a man couldn't escape no matter how hard he tried.

"Why you?"

"He said he was giving me a second chance to get it right." Cole's voice betrayed a touch of guilt, a hint of uncertainty.

"Get it right?"

"He said the last time he called, he had trusted me to do as he asked, and I failed."

"And what did he ask?"

"For me to take the message directly to you instead of going through channels."

Assistant Director Philip Crandall didn't speak right away as he watched an egret rise from the water and take flight, its wings flapping slowly as it glided across the flaming sky.

"Did I do the wrong thing?" Cole asked as the silence extended.

"Of course not," Crandall said. "You made the right call, Mr. Cole. I'll take care of it. Please don't discuss this call with anyone else."

He hung up the phone and took a couple of deep breaths. In and out, cleansing the tension from his neck and shoulders.

Finally. *Finally.*

He'd begun to think he'd never find a way to end the nightmare.

SON OF A BITCH.

Son of a *bitch*!

"What have I done?" Dallas Cole met his own gaze in the reflective glass of his office window. His office in the J. Edgar Hoover Building was little more than a closet with a single window he thanked his stars for every day, considering he'd started out in an even smaller closet without a window in sight. Support staff might be a vital cog in the FBI machine, but cogs didn't get corner offices and great views of— Well, okay, not many people at that ugly behemoth of a building had great views, period, despite FBI headquarters taking up prime property a hop, skip and a jump from the White House and other DC landmarks.

"Did you say something, Cole?"

The lilting female voice drew his mind out of self-imposed chaos and his gaze to the door. Michelle Matsumara, his supervisor, stood in the open doorway, neat and pretty in her trim blue suit.

"Talking to myself again, boss." He flashed a sheepish smile, feeling sick. Matsumara just gave a delicate shrug and continued down the hall.

He pressed his face into his hands. To say he'd been shocked by the phone call from a man claiming to be Cade Landry was an understatement of epic proportions. He'd spent the past year utterly certain Landry was dead and buried in some deep, dark hollow in the southern Appalachians.

Cole was from Harlan County, Kentucky. He knew all about deep, dark hollows.

Landry hadn't answered any of his questions, just told him to get it right this time. "Tell AD Crandall where he can meet me. And tell him I want him to come alone."

This time Cole had done as Landry asked. Bypassed Matsumara and her superior, Kilpatrick, and gone directly to Crandall, even though he knew, gut-deep, that both Matsumara and Kilpatrick were honest, trustworthy public servants—as good as they came, especially in a place like the capital.

After his phone call with the assistant director, Cole didn't think he could say the same of Crandall.

It hadn't been anything Crandall had said. His response had been everything anyone could have expected—an expression of concern about the contact from Cade Landry, reassurance that he'd done the right thing by calling him directly and, of course, an admonition to keep the call to himself.

But there'd been something else in Crandall's voice. Something as deep and dark as any hollows a man could find in the hills of Kentucky.

Cole looked at his office phone, his mind reeling. The phone Landry had used to make the call had apparently been equipped with number blocking, for the phone display had been blank. It wasn't likely redial would work, he thought, but he picked up the phone and tried it anyway.

Nothing happened.

Damn it, Landry. How could he warn the man about Crandall?

Would Landry even believe him? Nothing Crandall had said would strike anyone as suspicious. Hell, if Cole hadn't heard the man himself, he wouldn't have given a second thought to Crandall's responses.

Never ignore your instincts, boy. His grandmother's voice rang in his mind. Leona Halloran was a big believer in hunches and listening to the still, small voice in a person's head. "It's the warnin' voice of angels, Dallas. They're tellin' you, watch out! There's trouble ahead."

He pulled out his cell phone and stared at the

screen, thinking about his options. Who might know how to reach Landry after all this time?

The answer hit him like a gut punch. *Of course.*

He pulled up a search application on his phone and found the number he was looking for. As he started to dial it, the hair on the back of his neck rose, prickling the skin as if a cool finger had traced a path across the flesh.

Warning voices of angels, he thought, and shoved the phone back in his pocket. It was almost six o'clock on a Friday. Like most of the employees who worked in the J. Edgar Hoover Building, he didn't exactly watch the clock. But he'd worry about trying to impress management another day. He had a phone call to make.

And not from a phone that could be connected to him.

"Do you think he went straight to Crandall this time?"

Landry looked up at the sound of Olivia's voice. She stood in the open doorway of his bedroom, dressed for bed in a sleeveless T-shirt—the Atlanta Braves this time instead of Alabama. Her shorts might have hit midthigh on a shorter woman, but Olivia was a statuesque Amazon goddess, and there was enough skin visible to inspire some of his favorite fantasies.

"I have no idea," he admitted, dragging his

mind back to business. "I guess we'll find out tomorrow. Are Quinn and the others set for tomorrow?"

She nodded. "All set."

He patted the edge of the bed, well aware that he was wearing nothing beneath the sheet covering his lower half. He could tell by the flicker of awareness in her blue eyes that she was aware, as well.

But she crossed slowly to the bed and sat down beside him, facing him. Slowly, she reached out and pressed her palm against the center of his bare chest. "I guess this could be it. Freedom or—" Her throat bobbed as she swallowed the rest of the thought.

"I have to believe it's going to be a win. I think we've both earned one, don't you?"

Her fingers brushed over his chest muscles, lightly tracing the contours and sending delicious shudders down his spine. "I'm not sure wins can be earned. Not in a world this ruthless."

He curved his palm around her hip and saw, with visceral pleasure, the way her eyelids flickered at his touch. He could still affect her. Still elicit a physical response, deliver on the unspoken promise of pleasure.

"So it's all luck?" he asked in a growl, pressing his thumb against a point just below her hip bone that he knew could make her squirm.

Her soft gasp sent a jolt of raw desire racing straight to his core.

"Landry—" Her response ended on a soft groan as he flicked his thumb across the sensitive point again.

When he reached for her, she came willingly, her long limbs tangling with his. Her hips settled flush with his, and he was the one who groaned as his arousal amplified a thousandfold.

"I want you," he whispered against her throat.

She arched her neck as he flicked his tongue against the tendon just below her jaw. "You don't say."

Cupping her bottom, he positioned her more snugly over his sex. "Need proof?"

Her laugh was like cello music, deep and fluid. She stretched out, her body sleek against his, and he felt his heart begin to pound. "I was willing to take it on faith," she said, "but if you insist."

Suddenly, her hips began to vibrate against his, sending shock waves through his whole nervous system. In the middle of lowering her mouth to his, Olivia stopped short and growled an impressively profane word.

Pulling back until she straddled his thighs, she pulled her cell phone from the pocket of her shorts and glared at the display.

"Really, Quinn?" she snarled at the offending device.

"His sense of timing is really something to

behold," Landry murmured, trying to get his breathing back under control.

She answered the phone in a low, hostile voice. "What?"

Landry watched her expression shift from frustration to puzzlement. "Really. He called the agency?"

"What is it?" Landry asked.

"Hold on. I'm putting this on speaker so Landry can hear." She pulled the phone away from her ear and tapped the screen.

A moment later Quinn's voice came over the phone. "Cole called around six thirty, asking for you. We told him you were gone for the day and he flat out asked if you were with Landry."

Olivia arched her eyebrows at Landry. "And you responded how?"

"We told him we'd make sure you got his message."

"And did he leave one?"

"No. But we were able to get a trace on the number he was calling from. It's a gym not far from the National Mall. We haven't dug any deeper, but we'd probably find out that Cole is a member there."

"No, you wouldn't," Landry disagreed. "If he bothered to use a phone that doesn't belong to him, he'd use a number that isn't easily traced back to him. What we need to do is call him back on his cell phone."

"You think he'd answer?" Quinn asked.

"I think he'd have to chance it," Olivia said. "He called me for a reason. I don't think it's to catch up on my life these days."

"He thinks you know how to reach me," Landry said.

"He called for a reason. We need to find out what it is." She shifted until she was sitting on the bed instead of his thighs. Missing her warmth immediately, he stifled a sigh.

"Well, give it a try and call me back." Quinn hung up the phone.

Olivia edged closer to him on the bed until her hip was warm against his, as if she needed to be close to him as much as he needed to be close to her. "You have his number handy?"

Landry had it memorized. It had been the last phone number he'd dialed before the BRI had ambushed him, and he'd spent a good bit of his captivity repeating the number to himself to keep from thinking about his predicament.

He rattled it off to Olivia, who arched her eyebrows at his quick reply. But she didn't say anything as she dialed the number and put the phone on speaker so he could hear the call.

The phone rang four times before Dallas Cole's voice answered with a cautious "Hello?"

"You called," Olivia said bluntly.

"Right. I can't believe you actually called me back."

"Why did you call?" she asked, not bothering to hide her impatience. Olivia could be a sweet, considerate woman, but there were times when she could intimidate a bull moose. This was one of those times.

"Cade Landry called me."

"I know."

"He's with you, isn't he? I knew he would be."

"Why did you call back?"

"I did what he asked this time. I bypassed Matsumara and Kilpatrick and went straight to AD Crandall."

Olivia darted a look at Landry, clearly surprised. "What did he say?"

"He thanked me for telling him and said he'd handle everything as you asked."

"Well, that's good, then." Olivia frowned at Landry, clearly disappointed that Cole hadn't reacted as they'd thought he would. He wasn't happy himself. Now they'd have to figure out another plan—

"No, it's not." Cole's blunt tone interrupted Landry's thoughts. His accent, which usually was carefully neutral, held a strong hint of the Appalachian backwoods. "You and Landry thought I'd go through channels again, didn't you? That's why he called me again, even though the last time he came to me for help, he ended up in a hell of a tangle."

"Yes," Landry said.

"I'm sorry about that, man. You told me what to do, but I did it my way and you ended up paying for it. So this time, I did it your way. But Crandall's not what you think. He's not what I thought, either."

"But you said he agreed to handle it."

"He did. But I don't think he's going to—" Cole's words cut off on a soft expletive.

"What?" Olivia prodded.

"I've picked up a tail. At least I hope it's just a tail." His voice rose a notch, tight with tension. "Two sets of headlights, coming up fast."

"Where are you?"

"Driving south on 231, north of Ruckersville. Thought I should get out of town for the weekend— Son of a bitch!" His words were almost drowned out by the squeal of tires audible over the phone line.

Then the call cut off.

Olivia stared at Landry. "What just happened?"

Feeling sick, he reached for his phone. "I think Cole just got run off the road."

Chapter Seventeen

Mulberry Creek Diner wasn't nearly as picturesque as its name, but it offered Alexander Quinn the three things he was looking for in a staging point—lots of strong, hot coffee, free Wi-Fi and a large private room where eight men and four women could meet in relative privacy to discuss their plans to set a trap for a traitor.

"Still nothing from the Virginia State Police," Sutton Calhoun informed them after getting off the phone with his wife. "Ivy has a friend there who's promised to keep her informed if they get any accident reports from the Ruckersville area, but nobody's reported anything so far."

Almost twenty-four hours had passed since Dallas Cole's phone call had come to an abrupt end, and still no word about his whereabouts. Quinn didn't have a good feeling about Cole's chances for survival, but he was the FBI's problem. Quinn had his own agents to worry about.

"Maybe they weren't intending to kill him,"

Landry muttered. He was sitting near the end of the table, his chair pulled close to Olivia's, as if he didn't want to get too far away from her.

"Landry thinks someone might have taken him captive to question him," Olivia explained.

"Because that's what happened to you?" Nick Darcy asked. He sat to Quinn's left, McKenna Rigsby on his other side.

"Cole told me he didn't trust Crandall. He said something about their conversation made him feel really uneasy." Landry turned his coffee cup in circles in front of him. "I figure if a graphic designer's warning bells were going off during that conversation, an assistant director of the FBI might have had some suspicions, too."

"I wish there was a way to track Crandall. See if he's really on his way or if this is another wild-goose chase," Rigsby said.

"I'm working on that," Quinn said vaguely. Nobody asked him to elaborate. He wouldn't have done so if they had. He might not be in the spy business anymore, but he still knew what "need to know" meant. "I'm not sure it matters right now if Crandall shows up himself. To be honest, it's not that likely. You don't get to be an assistant director of the FBI if you do your own dirty work."

"Then what are we doing here?" Darcy asked, his dark eyes snapping up to meet Quinn's. "What do we think is going to happen?"

"We're setting a trap," Rigsby said.

"A trap Crandall's probably already seen through if he's sent people after Dallas Cole," Olivia muttered.

Adam Brand took a sip of coffee and grimaced. "We still run with our plan, in case that's where Crandall wants to make his stand."

"He won't," Olivia insisted.

Quinn didn't think he would, either. "He's put Dallas Cole on ice for a reason. What reason?"

"Setting up a new scapegoat?" That suggestion came from Seth Hammond, who sat across the table from Quinn. Covert Ops weren't his area of expertise, but he'd been in on this case from almost the beginning, tracking Landry and Olivia up the mountain and keeping an eye on them for Quinn. He'd wanted in on the finale, so Quinn had added him to the team.

"You mean, he wants to pin everything on Dallas Cole?" Rigsby asked. "But what about Landry? I thought he was already the designated patsy."

"Thanks, Rigsby." Landry made a face at her.

"You know what I mean. Crandall must know you suspect him by now. Or does he think you still believe he's one of the good guys?"

"I don't know. Maybe he sent people to grab Cole in order to keep him from communicating anything more to Olivia or me." Landry looked at Quinn. "Cole went to the trouble of not using a phone that could be connected to him. So Crandall may not know he's been in touch with us already."

"Wonder if Cole had reason to think he was under surveillance?" Hammond suggested.

"I think most people in the government assume their communications can be accessed easily. Especially someone in the FBI," Olivia said.

"And Crandall knows that." Quinn pushed away the half-drunk cup of coffee in front of him. "I think Olivia's right. Phil Crandall won't show his face here. That's not how this game is played."

"It's not a game," Landry muttered.

Quinn sighed. "You're right. Bad choice of words."

"You think nobody will show up at all?" Olivia asked.

"I didn't say that. Landry's a wild card, and if I were Crandall, I'd take one more shot at eliminating him. I'd be thinking, maybe Landry can't connect me to any of this mess, but what if he can? And I hate to say it, Olivia, but Landry is probably right about your being a target. Crandall must know by now that Landry's made contact with you."

"But if they know we're setting up a trap, why would anybody show up at all?" Hammond looked confused.

"They're not going to show up at the meeting point," Brand agreed. "We know that much already."

"But they'll do their own surveillance and go after Olivia and Landry once we close down the operation," Quinn explained. "This is a trap on top of a trap on top of a trap."

"Like running a long con," Hammond murmured.

"Sort of."

"I don't think we'll be able to prove Crandall was behind any of this just because someone tries to take out Landry and Sharp," Brand warned.

"No, but we may be able to finally bring some provable charges against some members of the Blue Ridge Infantry. Then the police can get search warrants, warrants to pull phone records, and maybe that will lead to even more warrants and searches—"

"*If* we can pull this off," Landry finished. "It's a big if."

"That could very well depend on the two of you," Quinn warned him. "We're going to have to fall back and leave you two exposed for a little while. I'm not going to lie and tell you it won't be dangerous. It will."

Landry's gaze shifted toward Olivia. "I don't think Olivia has to be part of the bait this time. She can fall back with you, and I can go it alone."

"No." Olivia shook her head. "Not happening."

"She's right." Quinn didn't like the idea of Olivia in the crosshairs, either. She was a good agent, a very good asset to his company, and he'd come to like and trust her during her time as one of his agents, as much as he ever allowed himself to trust anyone. "They almost certainly know you're together. They'll be very suspicious if you part company now."

"It's a chance I'm willing to take."

"I'm not," Olivia said. "This could be your best chance to clear your name and get your life back."

"If you're talking about the FBI, there's no way they'll take me back, even if I get out of this without criminal charges."

"There's more to life than working for the FBI." Olivia put her hand over Landry's, just a brief, firm touch, but in the gesture Quinn saw all he needed to know about where Olivia's loyalties ultimately lay.

Good thing they were chronically understaffed at The Gates these days. If everything worked out this afternoon, it looked as if he'd be adding a new investigator.

"We don't have time to fight this out," he warned. "We're an hour from meeting time, and the roads are still messy. We need to get rolling."

"I'm not leaving you, Landry. So deal with it."

Olivia's low, fervent tone left no room for argument. Landry met her gaze and sighed.

"Okay. Fine." He looked at the rest of the men and women at the table. "Let's get this party started."

Quinn pulled Olivia aside as they lined up to pay their dinner checks. "I meant what I said—our best chance to make this plan work is if you stick with Landry. But it's your choice. If you have any doubts…"

"I don't." Her chin lifted and her gaze met his without wavering.

"Good luck." He touched her arm and walked past her to the checkout counter, hoping this was one of those rare operations that went off without a hitch.

OLIVIA SUPPOSED THAT sometime in history, somewhere in the world, an operation had gone exactly as planned.

She'd just never been part of such a thing herself.

The meeting time had come and gone about an hour ago, and as they'd expected, Crandall had been a no-show. So had Dallas Cole or anyone from the Blue Ridge Infantry. But Seth Hammond had sent her a text message a few minutes ago to inform them the covert backup team had spotted about a half dozen men observing the meeting place from a distance.

Quinn and half the crew from The Gates were now headed back to the agency, while Landry and Olivia were on the road to Bryson City. The trip would take them through any number of potential ambush points, with only their stealthy backup team to help them out until more reinforcements could arrive.

By midnight, they'd passed almost all the potential ambush points the operation team had mapped out for them. They were five minutes from the Song Valley Music Hall and the Hunters' guest cabin.

"Do you think they figured out our plan?" Olivia asked as she forced herself to stay relaxed and focused.

"Check with the backup team."

Before she typed a letter, a text from Seth Hammond came in. "The men they've been following have just peeled off and seem to be heading back to Tennessee."

"I don't like this," Landry muttered.

Olivia didn't, either.

The Song Valley Music Hall was dark when they pulled into the driveway that wound past the restaurant toward the houses behind it. A couple of lights were still shining in upstairs rooms of the main house, but the guest cabin was dark and quiet.

Prickles of unease crept down Olivia's spine.

"Do you think the Hunters are still awake? There are lights on."

"What are you thinking?"

"I don't know," she admitted. "My danger radar is still going off like crazy, but I don't know if it's because I'm still on high alert from playing out this plan."

"I can't shake the feeling that it's not over," Landry admitted. "I don't trust that they've backed off tonight. Patience isn't something I've ever associated with the Blue Ridge Infantry."

Olivia felt sick. "And we've just put the Hunters in danger."

Without warning, Landry pulled the Tahoe to a stop in front of the Hunters' cabin and cut the engine. "We'd better tell them what's going on."

The sense of unease strengthened exponentially once they left the relative safety of the Tahoe and headed up the flagstone walk to the Hunters' cabin. The weight of the Glock tucked in the holster under her jacket was a partial comfort, but every instinct Olivia had was screaming warnings to stay on guard.

"Wait," she said as Landry started to reach for the screen door.

He glanced at her. "What?"

She reached in her pocket and pulled out the flashlight she'd carried with her on the operation. She flicked on the light and ran the narrow beam up and down the front of the screen door.

She was about to shut off the light when something glinted in the beam, catching her attention.

"Do not move," she said with quiet urgency.

Landry went still. "What did you see?"

"There's a wire sticking out between the door frame and the screen door. It might be a loose wire from the screen, but—"

"But it might be a trip wire."

"Right." She took a step backward. The floorboard beneath her boot gave a loud creak, and her heart skipped a beat.

A moment later she heard a muffled shout coming from inside. "Get away! The house is rigged!"

"That was Rafe," Landry growled, stopping his retreat. Olivia saw him eyeing the windows, looking for another mode of entry, but she had a feeling the windows might be rigged with explosives, as well.

She put her hand on his arm and pulled out her phone, punching in a message to Hammond. "We're not bomb-disposal experts. We can't get them out of there by ourselves."

"This is all my fault."

"No, it's not." Her phone vibrated and she checked the screen. Hammond's text in reply was blunt and profane. "He's informing Quinn. Quinn has contacts in the local law-enforcement agencies. He'll make sure the best bomb squad available shows up to take care of this situation. But we have to get away from this house." She turned toward the door and shouted, "Rafe! We're getting help. Hang in there!"

"The guest cabin's probably rigged, as well, in case we went there first," Landry growled.

"The music hall may be, too. We need to get the experts here before we make things worse."

Cade resisted for a moment when she gave his arm a sharp tug, but finally he turned and hurried her down the steps and back to the Tahoe.

As she reached for the door handle, something thudded hard against the front panel of the SUV just as she heard the crack of rifle fire echoing through the trees nearby.

"Get in the car!" Landry shouted, already opening the driver's door.

Olivia heard the click of the passenger door unlocking and jerked it open as another bullet shattered the side mirror in an explosion of flying glass. One small shard nicked her cheek with a sharp sting.

"Go, go, go!" She flung herself onto the passenger seat and jerked the door shut behind her.

Landry jerked the Tahoe in Reverse and whipped it around in a semicircle until they were facing the road.

Where three dusty pickup trucks blocked the driveway, each one manned guerrilla-style by men in camouflage standing in the truck beds, rifles aimed directly at them.

Chapter Eighteen

"Get down, get down!" Landry jerked the Tahoe in Reverse and swung into a sharp J-turn even as rifle fire split the night air. He heard more than saw Olivia hit the floorboard, putting three rows of seats between her and the shooters. She started speaking and he realized she'd called 911.

"We're taking rifle fire and we're hemmed in. I'm not sure there's any way to evade them." Olivia's voice was breathless and pitched a little higher than usual, but there was no sign of rising panic, no hint of fear taking over.

He wished he could say the same for himself. The mere thought of bringing in the authorities had his heart pounding and his mind reeling. He'd been stuck in fight or flight so long, the idea of turning over his fate to the authorities was almost more than he could fathom.

But they were out of options. Even as he swung the truck across the uneven yard behind the music hall, twisting the steering wheel back and forth to avoid the obstacle course between him and the other end of the music hall, he knew there was little chance of mistake. In the cracked glass of the rear window, he saw that only two of the trucks had taken up the pursuit, which meant the third vehicle was probably circling around to cut them off.

There was a small gap between the two trucks behind him, but if he timed it right—

He jammed on the brakes and the Tahoe's wheels slid on the lingering patches of melting snow as he jerked the wheel around to reverse course again and aimed for the narrowing gap between the two pickup trucks now barreling across the slippery ground straight at him in a terrifying game of chicken. Finally, as the grille of the Tahoe came a few short feet from the front of the trucks, the drivers swerved out to avoid a head-on collision.

The men in the truck beds were too busy clinging to the truck to get off any shots, and with a scrape of metal on metal as the SUV slid against the side of one of the trucks, the Tahoe shot the gap and raced up the driveway toward the road.

The trucks behind him had to avoid each other, slowing down their attempts to reverse course, and the third truck that had gone around the music hall to cut them off had no idea what had happened.

His heart pounding, Landry gunned the Tahoe

down the driveway, increasing his lead as he swung onto the road in front of the music hall and tore away from the pursuit.

Olivia had pulled herself up into the seat and was giving the 911 operator a play-by-play of what had just happened, peering through the gloom ahead to make out the sign on the next crossroad they passed. "We're still heading north on Valley Road, just past Soldier Junction." She listened a moment, turning around to look out the back. "They're still behind us but falling back. No, we didn't get any license numbers."

Suddenly, headlights came on, bright and blinding, from two vehicles parked on either side of the highway. Landry's heart jumped into his throat. "Son of a—"

Olivia's hand closed over his arm, and he darted a quick look at her.

"The Gates," she said, and he realized what she was telling him.

He drove past the two trucks parked on the shoulder and kept going. With a glance in his rearview mirror, he saw that the parked vehicles had pulled out behind him, blocking both lanes of Valley Road.

"They'll have vehicles trailing the trucks," Olivia said softly, the phone pressed against her chest. "They're going to hem them in."

"There'll be a firefight."

"Maybe. But those vehicles have bullet-resistant windows and armor. Just like this one."

Landry looked at the bullet holes in the rear window and realized they hadn't penetrated the glass. He released a harsh breath. "You could have told me."

"When?" She put the phone to her ear and told the 911 operator they'd evaded their pursuers and arranged for a meeting point with the sheriff's-department deputies responding to the call.

Landry eased the Tahoe to the shoulder where she indicated they should stop and put it in Park, though instinct told him not to cut the engine. Those jerks in the trucks weren't the only dangerous people in these hills.

"Are you okay?" He turned to look at Olivia, taking in her disheveled appearance and searching for any signs of injury. He saw a dark rivulet of blood running down the right side of her face. "You're bleeding!"

She reached up and touched her cheek, looking at the blood that came away on her fingers. "I got nicked by flying glass from the side mirror. Barely even stings. I'm fine. How about you?"

If he'd been injured, he couldn't feel it. He reached for her, tangling his fingers in the hair at the back of her neck, and pulled her across the gear console and into his embrace. Electricity seemed to flow through his veins like blood, sparking everywhere it traveled, until his whole body felt like a live wire, utterly on edge.

But slowly, as she lifted her hands to draw soothing circles across his back, the frantic energy ebbed, until he finally felt his pulse return to some semblance of normal.

Even the wail of sirens in the distance, moving inexorably closer, wasn't enough to jar his nervous system into another flight of panic. One way or another, his ordeal was over. The authorities would believe him or they wouldn't. But there would be no more running.

He might well be doomed to spend the next few years of his life behind bars, but he thought he could handle it now.

Now that Olivia was on his side.

"How much longer are they going to interrogate him?" Olivia couldn't stop her restless pacing beside Alexander Quinn. He sat with annoying calm in one of the two chairs that faced the empty desk of Ridge County Sheriff Max Clanton, who had insisted on observing the interview.

"You know the FBI. They like to swagger around and play the big dogs." The look Quinn shot her way was full of amusement, making her want to kick him in the shin with her hiking boots.

Instead, she stopped pacing, slumping in the chair next to him and stretching out her long legs, which had begun to ache. Dropping her chin to her chest, she glared at the empty desk chair and tried not to think about what Landry was going through in the interview room down the hall.

The Bryson City Police had picked up the men who'd been chasing Olivia and Landry, but so far, they hadn't been able to get much out of them. Quinn had told her it was possible they wouldn't be able to connect them to the Blue Ridge Infantry at all.

At least the Hunters had been safely rescued from their booby-trapped house. The bombs had been small pipe bombs, two hidden in the decorative urns on either side of the porch set to blow if anyone had opened a door or a window on the first floor. Fortunately, one of the officers on the Bryson City force had been an explosive-ordnance expert in the Marine Corps and had managed to disarm the simple explosives without incident.

But they still hadn't figured out how the men who'd accosted them had known to look for them in Bryson City at the Hunters' place.

"I get the feeling something's up with this interrogation," Quinn said a few minutes later, breaking the tense silence and drawing her thoughts back to the present.

"Good or bad?" She wasn't sure she wanted to hear the answer, but she couldn't go through life avoiding things that frightened her.

"I don't know. I just can't shake the sense something's changed."

She looked at him, trying to read his expression. A fool's game—Quinn never gave anything away he didn't want to. And sometimes when he wanted to, what he gave away was a lie he wanted you to believe.

Before she could ask another pointless question, the door to the office opened and Max Clanton entered, his sandy eyebrows lifting in surprise as he spotted them waiting in front of his desk. "Y'all know it's nearly five a.m., right? Figured you'd have moseyed on home for the night."

Olivia rose to face him. Max Clanton was a tall man, fit and trim, looking young for a man in his midforties, and from the handful of things she'd heard about his time on the Knoxville Police Force before he ran for Ridge County Sheriff, he was tough as a bull. But he must have seen something fierce in her expression when she turned to look at him, because his forward progress faltered and his expression shifted from affability to wariness.

"Where is Cade Landry?"

"I'm not sure." Avoiding her gaze, Clanton continued to his desk and sat in his chair, making a show of straightening the files on the corner of his desk.

"You're not sure?" she pressed, starting to

grow alarmed. "An hour ago he was in your interview room down the hall, talking to the FBI. I thought that's where you were, too."

"I was called away on a different case," Clanton said apologetically. "When I checked in again, the interview room was empty."

"Empty?" Olivia took a step toward the sheriff's desk.

Quinn rose and put his hand on her elbow, holding her in place. "Thank you for allowing us to wait in your office. If you have any further questions for Ms. Sharp or any of my employees, we'll be happy to oblige." He guided Olivia out the door and into the narrow corridor outside, shutting the door behind them.

"Where the hell is Landry?" she asked, keeping her voice down.

"My guess is, he's been taken into custody by the FBI, at least temporarily."

"And the Ridge County Sheriff's Department just let them take him?"

"Technically, he's committed no crimes in Ridge County that would give the sheriff primary jurisdiction." Quinn nudged her down the hall and out into the main foyer. "I'll make some calls, see if I can track down where he's been taken."

"That won't be necessary." A tall, dark-haired man with clear blue eyes and a Southern drawl stepped in front of them as they started toward the door. He handed Olivia a card.

It read "Will Cooper. Federal Bureau of Investigation." She looked up at him, her eyes narrowing.

"Where's Landry?"

"My guess is, he's currently on the way to The Gates. The FBI has released him under his own recognizance while the details of his situation continue to be sorted out." Cooper nodded at Quinn. "Nice to finally meet you, Mr. Quinn. I've heard a lot about you. I'm Will Cooper."

"One of the Alabama Coopers, I assume?"

Will smiled. "My brother Caleb gave me a call because I'm on a multistate task force investigating and interdicting domestic terror incidents. I've just been assigned temporary duty in the Knoxville field office to review some recent undercover operations run out of that office as well as the Johnson City resident agency."

"You got Landry released."

"He's got some details to work out, but unless different evidence arises, there aren't likely to be any charges pending against him." Will nodded toward the door. "I'd like to talk to you, Mr. Quinn, about your investigation into the Blue Ridge Infantry, if you'd be willing to discuss it with me."

Quinn looked at Olivia. She nodded. "Go ahead. I'll meet you there." She peeled off toward her car in the visitor's parking lot and pulled out her phone as she settled behind the steering wheel.

It was a long shot to think Landry would still have possession of the burner phone Quinn had given him. The cops had probably confiscated it as evidence. She'd just have to hope he was waiting for her.

When she arrived at The Gates, the agents' bull pen was buzzing with activity, agents making up for lost time after the snow days. Olivia caught Ava Solano's arm as the other woman edged past her in the doorway. Ava had worked with Landry briefly when they'd both been in the FBI's Johnson City RA. "Ava, have you seen Cade Landry?"

Ava's dark eyebrows lifted. "I thought he was at the sheriff's office, being questioned still. Did they let him go?"

"Seems to be the case, at least for now. Have you been here for the past hour or so?"

Ava nodded. "I have tons of paperwork I'm catching up on. If I see him, I'll tell him you're looking for him."

Olivia made herself slow down as she left the bull pen and headed for Quinn's office to see if he and Will Cooper had arrived. Maybe Cooper had misunderstood and the FBI agents who'd come from Knoxville to interrogate Landry had simply taken him to Knoxville for more questioning.

As disheartening an idea as it was to think he was still in deep trouble with the Bureau, it was a better option than the panicky fear starting to take up room in the back of her mind.

Face it, Olivia. There's always the chance he's run again.

But how would he run? He no longer had the Tahoe to drive. When he'd shown up in her front yard a few days ago, his only means of transportation was a thrift-store bicycle.

Which brought up another question. If he'd left the sheriff's department the way Will Cooper said, how had he managed it? On foot? Called a cab? Hopped on a bus?

She settled down in the chair in front of Quinn's desk and tried to think. Could he have caught a ride with another agent from The Gates? As far as she knew, she and Quinn had been the only ones there at the sheriff's office this afternoon, but Dennison's wife worked there as a deputy. She supposed Landry could have run into Dennison at the station and asked for a lift.

As she was dialing Dennison's number, Quinn and Will Cooper entered the office, their pace faltering a little when she stood and took a step toward them.

"Cooper, you said Landry had left and you thought he was headed here, but he's not here. Can you tell me how he left the sheriff's department?"

Cooper looked momentarily nonplussed by

the question, then apparently caught on to what she was asking. "One of the deputies going off duty offered him a ride."

"Male? Female?"

"Female. Dark hair, dark eyes, midthirties—"

That could fit Sara Dennison. "Thanks." She headed past them into the corridor and pulled out her phone. Sara's number was saved somewhere in her call list, wasn't it?

She found it as she was heading down the winding staircase to the first floor and made the call.

Sara answered on the second ring. "Dennison."

"Sara, it's Olivia. Did you give Cade Landry a ride this afternoon?"

"I did—he said he needed a lift to your place because he'd left a lot of his stuff there when y'all had to bug out. Frankly, he could do with a shower after sweating out an FBI interrogation, so I dropped him off at your cabin. I hope that was okay. I talked to Cain and he said you and Landry were friends."

"It's fine," Olivia assured her, already out the back door to the employee parking lot.

THE BICYCLE WAS still where Olivia had put it, in the small storage shed behind her cabin. The metal was icy cold but dry, protected from the snow by the sturdy shed's tin roof.

Landry ran his hand over the cold steel handlebars and remembered the ride up the mountain to this place, the snowfall increasing with every mile. He'd been terrified he was making the worst decision of his life.

He should have known better. Being with Olivia was always the right choice. How could he have ever thought anything different?

For a moment the sound of a car engine approaching up the mountain road sent a little ripple of alarm darting through him. But he made himself remain calm, though he didn't entirely relax his guard. He might not be stuck in fight-or-flight mode anymore, but there were still dangerous people out there who might be willing to take another shot at bringing him down.

The FBI hadn't given him back the Kimber or the Kel-Tec P-11 he'd had on him when they'd taken him in. He supposed they wanted to hold them as evidence until they fully settled his case.

That was fine. He had nothing to hide now.

Fortunately, he'd stashed his extra weapon in the locked cabinet in the shed, along with some ammo. He located the key in the hidden spot Olivia had shown him and unlocked the cabinet to retrieve the compact Ruger and its holster. He clipped the holster to his belt and loaded the magazine into the grip as the approaching vehicle came to a stop nearby. The engine cut, and he heard a door open, then close with a slam.

Olivia's voice rang out in the cold afternoon air. "Landry!"

He shoved the Ruger into the holster and edged through the shed door.

"Landry, are you here? Please say you're here!" The anxiety in Olivia's voice caught him by surprise, making him hurry as he rounded the side of the house toward her voice.

She was halfway up the porch steps when he reached the front yard.

"I'm here," he said.

She whirled around to look at him, her blue eyes wide. "Landry."

As he started to cross the yard, she came back down the porch steps and met him at the bottom. "Livvie."

She reached out and touched the front of his jacket, her gaze settling somewhere around the middle of his throat. "I thought you'd gone."

He put his hand over hers. Her fingers were cold and trembled a little beneath his touch. "You think I'd go without saying goodbye?"

She tugged her hand away and stepped back, her expression shuttering. "Is that why you're here? To say goodbye?"

"Let's go inside. Get a fire started and get warm." He put his hand under her elbow and nudged her toward the steps. She seemed to resist for a second, then gave in and went upstairs and unlocked her front door.

She went straight to the wood bin by the fireplace and went about the job of building a fire in the hearth, her movements quick and efficient, like everything she did.

She was radically competent, brilliantly resourceful and marvelously self-sufficient. She was, in short, a magnificent woman, and he could spend the rest of his life trying to be worthy of her without getting anywhere near his goal.

But he had to try. Because the alternative was walking away from her again. And he knew now, with utter certainty, that he didn't have it in him to do that again.

"I'm not sure my trouble with the FBI is over," he said, breaking the tense silence that had risen between them.

She gave the fire one last poke and turned around to look at him. "I really didn't expect them to let you go on your own recognizance, given that you've been a fugitive for so many months."

"I've offered to testify in front of a Senate subcommittee on domestic terrorism, which seemed to mollify my interrogators a bit." He moved closer, holding out his hands to warm them in front of the fire. "There was a new guy, Cooper— seemed to think I won't be charged with anything given the circumstances of my disappearance."

"That's good."

She still hadn't looked at him since they'd entered the cabin. Her shoulders were tense, her chin set and a little on the belligerent side.

"Livvie, I'm not leaving."

Slowly, she looked up at him. "You say that now…"

"I will never leave you again. Not if I have a choice. As long as you want me to hang around, I'm in. No doubts."

She raised one of her eyebrows a notch. "You? With no doubts?"

He caught her hands, tugged her around to look at him. In the firelight, she was a golden goddess, as beautiful and luminous a creature as he'd ever seen. His heart seemed to swell near bursting, so full of gratitude and love that he didn't know what to do with all the emotion.

"I lost you because I was a stupid idiot. But somehow, when everything seemed hopeless, I closed my eyes and looked for an answer, and there you were. Like a light in my darkness. So I found you. Because you were my hope. You're my home."

Her eyes glowed like jewels as she met and held his gaze. "Landry."

"I love you. I have loved you since almost the first day we met. There was never a point in time after that when I didn't love you, and there never will be." He touched her face, his thumb brushing against a sparkling tear that slid from one of her eyes. "So you tell me what you want."

"You." She slid her hand around his neck and pulled him to her. "I want you."

He kissed her then, a long, slow, intimate exploration that left them both breathless. Olivia finally broke away just enough to whisper against his mouth, "Say it again."

He didn't have to ask what she meant. "I love you."

Her answering smile was bright enough to light up the Eastern Seaboard. "Do you realize in all the time we were together, we never said those words to each other?"

He brushed her hair away from her cheek. "Technically, one of us still hasn't said them."

"I love you, idiot. If I didn't love you, I'd have probably shot you that first day you showed up in my front yard with that stupid bike."

"So let's do it, then."

She shot him a wicked look. "Do it? Here? Now?"

He laughed. "Well, yes, but I was actually thinking about getting hitched."

She took a step back, looking surprised. "Hitched?"

"Yeah. You know, married. Blissfully wed. Fitted with the old ball and chain."

"You were doing so well there for a minute."

He laughed again. "Marry me, Livvie." His

smile faded as he realized she might not have experienced the same epiphany he had about trust and devotion. "Unless you're still not sure you can trust me."

"No, that's not it." She brushed her thumb against his lip. "I just never thought I'd marry. I thought I'd be like my mom, always looking but never finding."

"Is that what you still think?"

She looked up at him, her gaze frank and open. "No, it's not. I know what I've found. I know it's worth keeping."

"So is that a yes?"

Her slow, sexy smile warmed him to his core. "Yes," she said and kissed him again.

Epilogue

The thin gold band on her left ring finger felt right, she decided after sneaking a peek for the sixth time in the past hour. It fit perfectly, neither loose nor constricting, as if it had been forged specifically for her alone.

"It's just a wedding ring," Landry murmured from his desk across from hers in the agents' bull pen on the second floor of The Gates. "It's not going to come alive and bite you."

She looked up at him, flashing him a quick, sheepish smile. "I like the way it looks. And the way it fits."

"I like the way it looks on you." The grin he shot back at her came with a full display of dimples and a softness in his green eyes that was endearingly shy.

She looked pointedly at the thicker band on his own ring finger. "Right back at ya."

"Oh, my God. Why didn't y'all just go on a real honeymoon instead of inflicting all this newlywed bliss on the rest of us?" Seth Hammond perched on the edge of Olivia's desk, shaking his head. "Have a little mercy on us, will ya?"

Sutton Calhoun thumped Hammond on the back of his head and dropped a file folder on Olivia's desk blotter. "I seem to remember a couple of months of you on the phone babbling disgusting endearments to your own bride, Hammond. Leave the newlyweds alone."

Calhoun waited for Hammond to wander back to his desk before he motioned Landry over. "Here's everything we could find on Dallas Cole. Any chance he's not a victim? Darryl Boyle hinted to Rigsby that he wasn't the only one in the FBI who was a true believer, and so far, we're just not finding any dirt on Philip Crandall."

"We just don't know," Landry admitted. "Given my own recent history, I'm in no position to assume a man's disappearance is evidence of his complicity in a crime. But Dallas Cole could have been trying to set us up so we wouldn't go to Crandall for help. It might have been a ploy to slow us down until the BRI could get their assets in place."

"Well, it's a place to look," Olivia pointed out. "If he *is* one of the bad guys, we need to find him."

Calhoun's slate blue eyes darkened. "And if he's not one of the bad guys?"

"Then he's in trouble and could use our help," Landry answered. "If he'll take it."

Olivia reached out, putting her hand over her husband's, her wedding band clinking quietly against his. His gaze flicked up to meet hers, and his dimples made a quick appearance.

A hint of amusement tinted Calhoun's voice. "Either way, Quinn wants us to find Cole and bring him in before the BRI gets their hands on him. He wants you two in charge of the investigation, since you know the most about him."

"We don't really know that much," Landry warned. "We could pick him out of a lineup, maybe, but—"

"We're investigators," Olivia reminded him. "It's our job to find out all we can about him now."

She picked up the folder Calhoun had placed on her desk blotter and opened it to the first page, a grainy photo of a dark-haired man with brown eyes and a guarded expression on his lean face. He was thirty-four, according to the notes clipped to the photos. Six foot one, approximately one hundred and eighty pounds, no distinguishing features.

"How does a graphic designer get mixed up

with a backwoods terror group?" she asked in a murmur.

"That's what we have to find out," Landry answered.

Olivia looked at the photo again, trying to see beyond the flat, expressionless surface of the image.

Who was Dallas Cole?

And which side was he really on?

* * * * *

Don't miss the other books in Paula Graves's miniseries THE GATES: MOST WANTED! *Look for them wherever Harlequin Intrigue books and ebooks are sold!*

LARGER-PRINT BOOKS!

HARLEQUIN *Presents*

GET 2 FREE LARGER-PRINT NOVELS PLUS 2 FREE GIFTS!

PASSION
SEDUCTION
GUARANTEED

HPLP15

LARGER-PRINT BOOKS!
GET 2 FREE LARGER-PRINT NOVELS PLUS
2 FREE GIFTS!

HARLEQUIN

Romance

From the Heart, For the Heart

LARGER-PRINT BOOKS!
GET 2 FREE LARGER-PRINT NOVELS PLUS
2 FREE GIFTS!

HARLEQUIN®

super romance®

More Story...More Romance

YES! Please send me 2 FREE LARGER-PRINT Harlequin® Superromance® novels and my 2 FREE gifts (gifts are worth about $10). After receiving them, if I don't wish to receive any more books, I can return the shipping statement marked "cancel." If I don't cancel, I will receive 4 brand-new novels every month and be billed just $5.94 per book in the U.S. or $6.24 per book in Canada. That's a savings of at least 12% off the cover price! It's quite a bargain! Shipping and handling is just 50¢ per book in the U.S. or 75¢ per book in Canada.* I understand that accepting the 2 free books and gifts places me under no obligation to buy anything. I can always return a shipment and cancel at any time. Even if I never buy another book, the two free books and gifts are mine to keep forever.

132/332 HDN GHVC

Name	(PLEASE PRINT)	
Address		Apt. #
City	State/Prov.	Zip/Postal Code

Signature (if under 18, a parent or guardian must sign)

Mail to the **Reader Service:**
IN U.S.A.: P.O. Box 1867, Buffalo, NY 14240-1867
IN CANADA: P.O. Box 609, Fort Erie, Ontario L2A 5X3

Want to try two free books from another line?
Call 1-800-873-8635 today or visit www.ReaderService.com.

* Terms and prices subject to change without notice. Prices do not include applicable taxes. Sales tax applicable in N.Y. Canadian residents will be charged applicable taxes. Offer not valid in Quebec. This offer is limited to one order per household. Not valid for current subscribers to Harlequin Superromance Larger-Print books. All orders subject to credit approval. Credit or debit balances in a customer's account(s) may be offset by any other outstanding balance owed by or to the customer. Please allow 4 to 6 weeks for delivery. Offer available while quantities last.

Your Privacy—The Reader Service is committed to protecting your privacy. Our Privacy Policy is available online at www.ReaderService.com or upon request from the Reader Service.

We make a portion of our mailing list available to reputable third parties that offer products we believe may interest you. If you prefer that we not exchange your name with third parties, or if you wish to clarify or modify your communication preferences, please visit us at www.ReaderService.com/consumerschoice or write to us at Reader Service Preference Service, P.O. Box 9062, Buffalo, NY 14240-9062. Include your complete name and address.

HSRLP15

YES! Please send me **The Montana Mavericks Collection** in Larger Print. This collection begins with 3 FREE books and 2 FREE gifts (gifts valued at approx. $20.00 retail) in the first shipment, along with the other first 4 books from the collection! If I do not cancel, I will receive 8 monthly shipments until I have the entire 51-book Montana Mavericks collection. I will receive 2 or 3 FREE books in each shipment and I will pay just $4.99 US/ $5.89 CDN for each of the other four books in each shipment, plus $2.99 for shipping and handling per shipment.*If I decide to keep the entire collection, I'll have paid for only 32 books, because 19 books are FREE! I understand that accepting the 3 free books and gifts places me under no obligation to buy anything. I can always return a shipment and cancel at any time. My free books and gifts are mine to keep no matter what I decide.

263 HCN 2404   463 HCN 2404

Name	(PLEASE PRINT)

Address	Apt. #

City	State/Prov.	Zip/Postal Code

Signature (if under 18, a parent or guardian must sign)

Mail to the **Reader Service:**

IN U.S.A.: P.O. Box 1867, Buffalo, NY 14240-1867
IN CANADA: P.O. Box 609, Fort Erie, Ontario L2A 5X3